THE SECRETS *of the* SAFFRON MOUNTAIN

BY

MARK AKST

The Secrets of the Saffron Mountain

Copyright © 2024 by Mark Akst

Printed in the United States of America

Hardcover ISBN: 978-1-965253-02-1
Paperback ISBN: 978-1-965253-03-8
Ebook ISBN: 978-1-965253-04-5

Canoe Tree Press

Canoe Tree Press is a division of DartFrog Books
301 S. McDowell St.
Suite 125-1625
Charlotte, NC 28204

www.DartFrogBooks.com

Other Novels in the *Mark Cohn* Series
by Mark Akst

King Herod's Treasure
The Mossad Warrior Spy

TABLE OF CONTENTS

CHAPTER 1

REVELATION

As I swung on a rope line attached to my harness 300 feet (91.5m) above the Negev desert floor and more than 300 feet (91.5m) down from the top of the ridge on Mount Karkom, I thought to myself, "What is a nice Jewish boy doing in a place like this? Am I nuts?" I braced myself with my two feet against the almost perpendicular cliff rock face. I was having second thoughts about this whole expedition to prove once and for all that Mount Karkom was actually the biblical Mount Sinai. The cool December desert wind had turned cold—chilling me—and was getting stronger. What was pleasantly cool weather on the ground had turned cold, swinging in the breeze 300 plus feet (91.5m) above it.

I must have been insane when I had insisted on rappelling off the 600 foot (183m) high ridge face of the mountain's plateau myself. But I have more than a million dollars in cost riding on the success of this expedition and I am not folding my tent and leaving before I do this one last check.

Although now I have an equally strong feeling that it might be the last thing I ever do! When the team recently searched the ground below, we found nothing but a few scratches in the rock at the base of Mount Karkom. Indeed, I could clearly see from this high vantage point the indentations in the ground that I thought had been the remains of an ancient road dead-ending into the side of Mount Karkom. But I now could also see the other end of these indentations in the ground, which surprisingly stopped abruptly at the edge of the ancient dry riverbed that had once flowed in the middle of the valley in front of the mountain. I just wanted to make sure before we abandoned the expedition that no stone was left unturned, so to speak, by checking the upper reaches of the mountain above the supposed road tracks.

From my perch here, however, I did notice evidence of the top edges of an ancient landslide that had covered the area directly below me. This confirmed what Sam had previously found with his solid rock penetrating LIDAR electronic equipment. We were all here based on my brief observation, which I had made when I had previously stood on the top of the mountain ridge. The angle of the sun revealed shadows on the ground, which looked like it was once a road dead ending into the mountain. I made this observation the first time I visited with my then Israeli guide, now married partner, Eric

Jansen. Thus, my hunch was that the extension of this road could lead into a long-forgotten cave inside the mountain. And inside the cave, there could be items that could possibly prove Mount Karkom, located here in the Negev Desert, was actually the holy biblical mountain called Sinai.

At least that was my hunch or theory. Also, this was going to be some expensive mistake on my part. I had assembled a team which included myself, Mark Cohn—older in body but young in spirit; Eric Jansen, my handsome, younger partner and expert archeologist; Sam Reichman, the president of the GPR company whose advanced scientific methods of looking through solid surfaces were vital to an archeological dig, and physically strong as a bull; Ariel Kurtz, our young expert in all things video and the official expedition cameraman/photographer and as classically and darkly handsome as my Eric was blond; also Ariel's new wife, Julie, a stunning redhead and his technical assistant in filming our expedition; and lastly the newest member of our team, Asher Ben-Levy, older brother of Moshe Ben-Levy, who had been our guide on the Temple Mount in Jerusalem.

Asher was also a trained archeologist and an ordained orthodox rabbi. He was the only one of the team to wear a yarmulke (also called a skull cap by the Catholic Church). He was 50 years old with brown eyes and grayish brown hair. He was also the only one of the team to sport a beard, which, in my opinion, was way too long and unkempt. Both Sam and Eric insisted on him joining the team. They told me various ministry heads in Jerusalem (but did not say which ones) thought it best we take him with us this time to prevent any minor missteps like we had on our last expedition since many people consider Mount Karkom a holy site. It was working fine so far since we hadn't found anything. Moreover, Asher had a great sense of humor and loved to cook. He had become the expedition's unofficial chef! We have all been eating kosher food now—since he controlled the kitchen and also happened to be a really good cook.

In addition to the team, we had access to two Chinook helicopters and luckily two young enthusiastic crew members who were also amateur archeologists and volunteered to stay and help between their helicopter trips to transport us and our equipment—tents, etc. These helicopters were loaned to us by the Israeli military, avoiding a grueling three-hour jeep ride—half of it off-road—across an unforgiving Negev desert from Be'er Sheva (Israel's regional capital of the Negev). Moreover, using the helicopters, our trip time was cut from Hatzor Air Base in Central Israel to less than an hour by helicopter from there to the military training base the government let us use near Mount Karkom. And then on from there, a short jeep ride to our base camp in the valley in front of Mount Karkom. Moreover, our two volunteers from the military were really helpful in setting up our camp. Thanks to them, we all got an exciting bird's eye view of the mountain and nearby desert terrain while flying around our campsite the first day. Our deal with the military was we only had to reimburse the military for the cost of the fuel.

The money for all this was funded by Jacob Kurtz, the father of our team member Ariel Kurtz. Jacob was an Israeli multi-millionaire film producer and promoter and had funded our previous expedition. All this was based on my hunch from our first visit that Mount Karkom was the biblical Mount Sinai of the Exodus. However, I was well aware that this was a gamble, notwithstanding that all my previous hunches or insights or whatever you want to call them had proven correct.

Yes, a gamble, but also, the fact that in the entrance to a cave halfway up the cliff face of the mountain, since Paleolithic times, during the winter solstice around mid-afternoon, the rays of sunlight light up the rear of a jagged rock sitting at the entrance, reflecting light in a circle around the rock and the whole front of the cave. I had seen photos of this phenomenon. And yes—to my doubting, secular eyes, it most definitely looked like the burning bush of

Mount Sinai of the Exodus! Regardless of what we find, I will wait two more days to see this with my own eyes. Perhaps seeing this in person can somehow give me an idea of how to salvage this expedition. In the meantime, I am hanging off the side of the cliff face of the mountain. And I had another hunch!

I am so close to the entrance of the cave in the mountain with the craggy round rock that in two days will become the burning bush. Why not swing over and stand there and look in? I don't think anyone has ever done this except maybe Moses! So, without thinking it through, I began swinging back and forth on my rope, using my legs to propel myself off the mountain and closer and closer to the hole in the mountain face. I was swinging back and forth, using the climbing rope like a fulcrum. Eric, my partner, was more than 300 feet above me, controlling my rope pulley apparatus. He immediately saw what I was doing and started yelling down at me to stop, as it was too dangerous. Sam Reichman, our GPS expert and built like a bull, also saw what I was doing from 300 feet (91.5m) below me. Next to him was Ariel, our cameraman, who filmed everything. Sam immediately tried steadying the end of my rope dangling on the ground. I think I also heard him yell for me to stop. But once I get a thought in my head, there is no stopping me.

With each swing, I got closer and closer to the area where, in the Bible, the Lord God appeared to Moses as a burning bush that was not consumed, and where the Ten Commandments were written. My heart was pounding. I could almost see inside. Almost, that is. As I was stepping off the cliff face as lightly but forcefully as I could while hanging onto my rope, I kept noticing the ridges in the rock face getting deeper and longer as I got closer to the opening. On my final swing, I noticed something long, black, and shiny laying in the ridge crevice. It was a black Sinai cobra that raised its head in a strike position as I was swinging closer. I instantly dug the heels of my desert boots hard on the rock face to stop myself in full swing. Luckily, I came to a full stop just before the cobra struck, missing my neck by an inch. But it came close enough for me to smell its scent and hear its hiss. It smelled like death.

Needless to say, I backed up as fast as I could. As I was backing up just in front of this recoiled cobra, I noticed more of them pouring out of the famous burning bush hole that I was so eager to explore. They were all quickly slithering over the rock cliff ridges, heading straight towards me. Backtracking to the middle of the fulcrum, where my rope would hang straight down, seemed to take an eternity, yet I was moving as quickly as I could. I was so upset that I must have loosened my grip on my rope and started sliding down too fast. I was wearing thick gloves to avoid getting rope burn while climbing—Eric had insisted I wear them. One of his hobbies is mountaineering, and he told me gloves like these had saved his hands more than once from rope burn. He was right. I could feel the heat of the ropes through my gloves as I struggled to slow myself down. I think I managed to slow down a little bit. I was descending so fast that my favorite brown fedora, an Indiana Jones-style hat, flew off. It was a present from my team given to me on our last expedition. Moreover, I hadn't fully realized at the time, but both Sam and Eric had been watching every step of my high-flying act (or ordeal, to me).

It took seconds for me to descend, and the next thing I remember, I was in Sam's arms. He must have caught me before I hit the ground and broken both legs or worse! He just looked down at me in his arms and said, "Having a bad day? But I got you and you're fine!" With that, he swung me around so I could stand on my own two feet. He did, however, continue to hold me tight around my waist with his left hand so I could grab onto his right shoulder while trying to stand and regain my balance. Even Ariel, standing close to us, stopped filming for a second to ask if I was okay.

Less than two minutes later, while I was still dizzy from my fall, the six-foot black Sinai cobra that had been chasing me landed with a thud right in front of us. You would think a fall like that would kill it, but not that tough old snake! It immediately coiled in a strike position. As it made its lightning-fast strike towards me, I heard Sam unsnap his large military style knife that he carried in a knife holster attached to his belt with his free right hand. I had previously questioned him when we first arrived here on why he always carried such a large knife. At that time, he casually said you never know what you're going to run into in the deep desert. He now caught the lightning-fast strike of the cobra with an even faster swing of his knife, so quick that he severed the cobra's neck just behind its head mid-strike. I heard the cobra's head fall to the ground and saw its mouth and fangs clicking between my feet. Its extended fangs harmlessly ejecting poisonous venom onto my boots and pants. As I looked up, I saw the cobra's body writhing and coiling itself in pain. The open wound where its head had been spewing red blood everywhere. When I felt its surprisingly hot blood sprayed across the back of my hand, my eyes rolled back in my head and I fainted. Thank God that Sam was still gripping my waist with his left hand, so I didn't join the snake on the ground!

Strangely, when I fainted, I could no longer see anything and had no power in my limbs but I could still hear. I heard Ariel say, "What a great shot. I got it all!" while Sam said that it was the biggest Sinai cobra he had ever seen. Meanwhile, Eric had been watching what was happening from more than 600 feet(183m) up on the edge of the ridge of Mount Karkom. With his mountaineering skills of a natural born sportsman, it took him less than two minutes to jump over the side of the cliff and rappel himself down to the ground and run over to us. He was in such great shape that he wasn't even breathing hard when he got to us. But I am sure the look on his face must have been that of extreme worry.

As he approached, Sam said to him, "I think this is yours! But he's fine—just fainted." Then he unloaded me into Eric's arms. All Eric said was, "I better take him back to our tent and have him checked out." With that, he swung my limp body over his shoulder, holding my two legs tightly in front of him and letting the rest of me dangle behind him. Then he started to walk briskly back to our tent about a quarter of a mile away but still in the valley in front of Mount Karkom. Ariel, as usual, followed and filmed.

Since I was dangling head down and arms also extended down, my blood started to return to my head, my eyes rolled back to where they were supposed to be, and my strength began to return to my limbs. So, when I opened my eyes, the first thing I saw was Eric's two round bouncing buns inches from my face but upside down. So I reached out and grabbed those two hard, rounded melons, trying to push myself into a more upright position. When I did this, Eric loudly said he could tell I was feeling better! "But for now, relax and enjoy the view. We only have a little way to go to get you back to our tent." Actually, I was just trying to see where my hat had gone. Luckily, I saw Sam holding it. I was relieved that I had not lost it.

By the time we got back to the tent, Sam had already alerted the entire team by cellphone to what I had done and what had just happened because of it. First thing back in the tent, Eric laid me gently down on my cot. As my total senses returned, I felt so embarrassed (and old) that I had caused this emergency and had been treated like a sack of potatoes by two of the most perfectly fit men I had ever met. Both tough IDF and Mossad trained warriors who also had to babysit me!

Surprisingly, Julia, Ariel's new wife and technical assistant, took over what was happening next in our tent. I hadn't known this, but she had been a nurse in the military. She now started field triage on me, which she had done dozens of times before in the IDF. I started to protest that I felt fine, but she basically told me to shut up and be still.

The whole team, including Sam and our rabbi and cook Asher, was now in our tent. It was getting crowded, and everyone had something to say. Julie finally pronounced me normal (for me—LOL), and I noticed the anxiety level in the tent lowered a bit. She said I just needed some rest. Before I totally relaxed, however, I was curious about one thing. I asked Sam, who by now was also in the tent, "What was a black Sinai cobra doing in the Negev?" He responded in his most professorial tone that the delineation between the Negev desert and the Sinai Peninsula was political, but the climate, animals, and native flora and fauna were the same in both places, and that there was no such delineation in the time of Moses. He also added that just because the tall border fence between Egypt and Israel runs very close to Mount Karkom, it had nothing to do with where black Sinai cobras choose to live.

Next, Asher, assuming his official rabbi's role, commented that my attempt to enter the entrance to the cave where the burning bush was said to appear was strictly off-limits and illegal. Our military permit to explore and potentially excavate in this military reserve area did not include it. Many considered it a holy site, and trespassing was forbidden. He expressed his anger, reminding me of the warning the Prime Minister had given me after my last expedition—no more favors. Violating Israeli archeological laws again would result in jail time for me, and possibly for the rest of the team as my accomplices. My first reaction to this was how the heck did he know about my conversation with the Prime Minister, but then remembered that sooner or later in Israel everyone eventually knows everything about everyone. He must have researched me thoroughly before joining the expedition. Despite his remarks, I did recall hearing something about a prohibition against entering the cave on Mount Karkom.

Noticing the team's concern, Asher lightened the mood, asking if I wanted to hear the good news. I agreed, and he said that since I hadn't actually entered the cave, no laws were broken. So he continued by joking about making cobra kebabs for dinner, claiming they tasted like chicken. The whole team groaned at the thought.

However, I wasn't going to let his joke slide. I told him I knew he was joking because snakes slither on the ground and therefore were not kosher. And since he was an orthodox rabbi, I knew he only cooked kosher meals. Surprised, he asked how a secular Jew like myself knew which food was kosher and which was not.

To this I responded in Hebrew, which shocked the entire team except Eric, who had been helping me learn it. Yes, I was studying modern Hebrew and getting pretty good at it. And also added that I was also in the process of reading the Torah in its original language, understanding exactly what Moses said about dietary restrictions without needing a translation. Upon hearing this, Asher's tone became more respectful, confirming that snakes were not kosher and would not be served for dinner. Everyone in the room sighed in relief when he said this.

As Asher turned to leave, he suggested that maybe I should ponder this thought that the snake might not have been a deadly creature I had almost accidentally stepped on, but a guardian placed there by God to protect His holy site, which I had nearly violated. His parting comment struck me as a revelation that what he had just said was true. Upon hearing his comment, the entire team fell silent, as if pondering the idea themselves.

Julie broke the silence by loudly insisting everyone leave the tent to let me rest. Everyone left except for Eric who sat by my bed and tightly held my hand as I lay back on my cot. As I drifted off to sleep, I realized that by holding my hand he was trying to share his strength with me. I felt it flowing into me and had a premonition that I would need it in the days to come.

CHAPTER 2

THE LEVITE PRIEST

After what I had just experienced, I hadn't realized how truly tired I was. I slept through dinner that night and awakened early the next morning feeling refreshed and ready for the day. Eric was sound asleep on his cot next to me. Not wanting to disturb him, I quietly left our tent. Outside, I deeply breathed in the cool desert morning air and delighted in the desert solitude. I think I also detected a little moisture from the early morning desert dew. The air smelled sweet. I then made a beeline to our port-a-potty that our helicopter crew had conveniently dropped off for the team to use. I washed my hands and the sleep off my face in our makeshift outdoor sink, which was more like an extended hose. After that, I went directly to our mess hall tent. My appetite had come roaring back.

As I entered the tent, I saw the newest member of our team, Rabbi Asher Ben-Levy, already cooking breakfast. I knew him well enough by now to know that no one got in his way when he was cooking! So, I politely asked him when breakfast would be ready, as I was starving. He said he was glad that I was feeling better and to sit down; his famous Israeli breakfast buffet would be ready in a couple of minutes. Israel is known for its delicious buffet breakfasts, which consist of yogurts, cheeses, salads, omelets, peppers, flatbreads (pita), dips, and butter. Asher's specialty was homemade hummus, which was delicious, and my favorite shakshouka, which consisted of eggs floating in a homemade fresh tomato sauce with plenty of garlic and onions, served hot with bread on the side for dipping. This buffet style of breakfast had originated on the collective kibbutz years ago.

The buffet was served on a long table against the tent wall. When Asher put the shakshouka down on the table, I couldn't wait any longer and went to the buffet table, serving myself. I returned to my seat with a full plate and started to eat with gusto. Asher returned to the kitchen side of the tent to finish cutting some bread.

It was still just me and Asher in the tent when he said to me in a most sanctimonious tone that I should be ashamed of myself for trying to enter the hole where the burning bush appears. He then said I was a bumbling amateur archeologist and sodomite who had walked on sacred ground and had almost violated a most holy site. He warned me to be more careful in the future.

With this comment, I stopped eating. I had made considerable effort later in my life to become a kinder, gentler person, especially now that I had a gorgeous life partner who loved me and whom I loved dearly. However, in my early life, I had my share of neighborhood street fights on the mean streets of New York City and had successfully won more than one. I had kept this anger buried and safely locked away for many years now. Almost instantly, I felt that anger bubble up in me again—an anger that was hard to control. I didn't mind that he called me a bumbling amateur archeologist. He was correct there. However, I would have added the word "lucky" as well. What stuck in my throat was his use of the word sodomite in such a sanctimonious tone. I surprised myself with my cold, controlled response, pointing out that the only people who would give a damn was the Chief Rabbinate, "a bunch of old men who you can smell before you can see and who want to send Israel back to a time of ignorance." I ended my response with the most studied half-smile smirk on my face I could muster. It hit its mark. Asher was enraged. He responded that he was the Chief Rabbinate's representative here and I should best take what he said seriously. I noticed he had changed the way he was holding his bread knife from a cutting position to a stabbing position. I thought to myself, "He wants to play? Then let's play." I instantly knew that the metal breakfast chair on the other side of the table from where I was sitting would not only make a good defense against his knife, but if I pushed over the table to get to it fast enough, I could crush his skull with it before he had time to think or move out of the way. I would send him back in a box!

However, in the next second before I could blink, Sam Reichman, that huge bull of a man, was sitting in my metal chair potential weapon! All he said, looking straight at me, was, "Good morning and Shalom to everyone." Of all the chairs in the mess hall tent, he picked the one that placed himself strategically between me and Asher. That was no accident. Then I also sensed Eric had entered the tent, positioning himself directly behind me. I was sure they both noticed the fighting tension in the tent between Asher and me. Next came Ariel and Julie, followed by the two young, enthusiastic helicopter pilots who had volunteered to help us with the grunt work during our expedition.

I knew I had to get control of myself but it was going to be difficult. Then Eric quickly picked me up and swung me around pinning my arms to my sides with a giant hug and said loudly so everyone could hear, "I didn't get my morning kiss yet." I gave him a perfunctory kiss on the mouth by which Eric knew instantly something was not right with me. Ariel then yelled, "Get a room." Everyone laughed except Asher, who was also composing himself. I used the opportunity while my cheek was pressed against Eric's to whisper that Asher worked for the Chief Rabbinate of Israel. Eric softly replied directly into my ear, "We know. Calm down."

As Eric released me from his bear hug, I sat down again facing Sam. I was now in control of myself, so the first thing I said to Sam was that I hadn't had the chance yesterday, but I wanted to thank him for saving my life. Sam simply looked at me with a warm smile on his face and said, "I actually saved you twice yesterday." I thought about this for a moment and said he was right. I owed him my life twice over. All Sam said in response was, "You're welcome. Now let's eat." Everyone in the room ate hungrily, including me. Except I couldn't help keeping a half an eye on Asher.

After wolfing down my breakfast I needed to further clear my head, so I excused myself to spend some time alone outside, but asked everyone if they could attend a planning meeting in about thirty minutes here in the mess tent. Everyone agreed and thought it was a good idea. As I walked out of the tent, I heard Sam say to Eric that Eric owed him one shekel. Later, I learned that apparently, they had bet how long it would take for Asher and me to have a fight. Sam bet two days and he won! I hate being so predictable.

As I stepped outside the tent situated at the valley's entrance before Mount Karkom's burning bush hole, the overwhelming, mysterious, ancient power of this place enveloped me again. I felt a power almost metaphysical—as if God Himself was here. I had first sensed it the moment I disembarked the helicopter two days prior. But the closer I got to the burning bush hole in the mountain, the stronger the feeling grew. This sensation was intensifying as we approached the winter solstice date, which was the next day. I think the whole team felt it too, but not as much as I did. It had caused Eric and me to lose interest in making love, as if we had become virgins again. As I continued to walk around our deserted camp with the mess tent's noise fading, an idea struck me. We hadn't yet thoroughly explored the plateau on top of Mount Karkom where there were thousands of petroglyphs. So, I thought it would be productive for the team to spend the rest of the day on the plateau above us studying its many petroglyphs carved into the rock thousands of years before the time of Moses. As for myself, I really didn't know what I would be looking for, but I was sure I'd recognize it when I saw it. Besides, we hadn't made any groundbreaking archeological discoveries yet. Perhaps the time spent up there would help me figure out what to tell Jacob Kurtz who funded this expensive expedition based only on my hunch from a previous visit.

I took my time walking back to our mess tent which would now serve as our meeting hall. When I entered, everyone was nearly done helping Asher clean up from breakfast. I sat there patiently, still a little embarrassed about my experience on the mountainside yesterday. Soon, everyone was seated and ready to start our meeting. As usual, Ariel began filming.

I started by thanking everyone for their hard work and support so far, asking them to interrupt me if I forgot anything. I reviewed what the expedition had accomplished so far, noting that we had arrived two days ago early in the morning by two helicopters on loan from the IDF. We had received permits from the military to explore Mount Karkom and its nearby surrounding area. These permits were rarely given due to the area's proximity to the Egyptian border and its location within a major Israeli military training reserve. Sam Reichman and Eric Jansen's political and military connections, as well as my serendipitous meeting with the Israeli Prime Minister at one of Jacob Kurtz's parties, helped us secure the permits. Jacob's generous funding and high-level ministerial contacts sealed the deal. Moreover, this part of the Negev was rarely open to tourists, except for a week during the winter solstice and one week around Passover in the spring.

After expressing my gratitude to everyone involved, I continued with a review of our initial aerial trip by helicopter over Mount Karkom. This gave us an excellent overview of the area before we landed. Everyone on our team helped unload our gear and then we all went directly to the site on the side of the mountain that I thought would lead to a hidden cave or chamber inside the mountain. We spent the rest of the first day exploring and testing the area, where I had seen indentations in the ground that looked like an ancient road leading into Mount Karkom's side. Sam, president of our GPR company, shared that he had not known what would be needed to penetrate the mountain's secrets so he brought several types of equipment with him: first was his GPR equipment which stands for ground-penetrating radar, next, LIDAR equipment for scanning solid surfaces using laser radar sensors and, lastly, the most advanced state-of-the-art laser scanning equipment available.

Sam used the GPR sensors in a small area to view the ground between the two visible indentations, which formed a trail that clearly led towards the ancient dry river bed from the mountain's side. He found nothing underneath the supposed ancient road—no man-made stones for a road or impacted earth, just natural limestone rock. He then turned his attention to the side of the mountain and determined that the best way to see into it was to use his most advanced laser scanning equipment. However, after setting it up, Sam's conclusion was that the sensors found the side of the mountain to be deceptive; it appeared solid but was actually covered in five feet of loose rock from an ancient landslide. Beyond that layer, the sensors had penetrated an additional twenty feet of solid rock. Sam concluded that there was no cave or opening beyond this wall of rock.

Concurrently, Eric had surveyed the entire area with his trained archeologist eyes. He came to the same conclusion. He also found nothing. Also, during this time on our first day, Asher and our two helicopter pilots had continued to do some final set ups for our campsite. However, they too soon heard we had all come up empty. Our first day of exploration based on my hunch about an ancient road leading to a cave was disappointing. The only person who seemed happy at dinner that night was Asher; the rest of us ate in near silence.

Our second day proved to be even more frustrating. Not ready to give up, I decided to rappel down the 600 foot (183 m) high ridge off Mount Karkom to explore the area where the ground indentations were located. With Eric and Sam's help, I learned how to use their mountain climbing equipment and faced my fear of heights. Sam ended up saving my life twice: first, catching me when I descended too quickly, and then moments later from a monstrous snake. And just for the record, that snake was only the second scariest thing that happened to me the day before. The first was getting my body to go over that cliff to rappel down on that skinny rope! And I also wanted to thank everyone else for their support and help when I fainted too. After I said this everyone smiled and said they were glad I made it. I humbly added that unfortunately the only thing I found by rappelling down the mountain was that there were signs of an ancient landslide which confirmed Sam's findings.

So, I continued that today I would like the team to research the plateau on top of Mount Karkom, which was adorned with numerous petroglyphs and upright ancient stone monuments. I informed the team that we would make a decision about the future of our expedition the morning after the winter solstice. We would all still get to witness the burning bush phenomenon tomorrow, regardless of our discoveries.

After flying to the plateau by helicopter, we spent the day exploring the area, filled with thousands of ancient rock engravings in an approximately four-and-a-half square mile area. One of the most fascinating items for me were the dozens of cult sites—especially one with an altar consisting of twelve standing stones around a circle. Could it possibly represent the twelve tribes? Nearby was a rock surface carving of ten boxes arranged in a tablet formation. Could it represent the ten commandments? My hunch was yes to both. The sense of human history here was palpable. However, I couldn't shake the feeling that I was still searching for something.

The petroglyphs depicted geometric lines, symbols or animals. The animals were of various animal species such as deer, birds, lions, and antelope. These rock art drawings proved to me that thousands of years ago this area was once well-watered and not a desert. Indeed, it was very well watered to support big animals like those drawn. Archeologists estimate these drawings to be from the Neolithic period, making them roughly 10,000 years old by the time Moses arrived here. I suspected that this had been a cult site for even longer, perhaps dating back to when humanoids first walked the earth—hundreds of thousands of years ago.

And then, there it was. What I had come here to find. It was a rock carving of a single eye. I knew instantly it was meant to represent the Eye of God. It was situated apart from the other art, almost as if the surrounding natural rocks were forming an altar entrance. As I made my way towards the drawing, my mind was a whirlwind of questions. Who had created this? When? And why?

The first peculiar thing I noticed about the drawing of this solitary human eye was its remarkable clarity. It was as vivid today as the day it was created. " How odd?" I thought. The art had seemingly defied the ravages of time. The question in my mind was: "Wasn't this supposed to be the mountain of the burning bush, not an eye?" More importantly, as I drew closer to the rock carving of the eye, an uncanny sensation began to fill me. The line between the tangible and the mystical seemed to blur. I was overwhelmed by its power, and I had to remind myself that this was no dream. The realization that I was alone in this section of the mountain added to my unease. It was also getting late. I decided to stop in my tracks and not approach the petroglyph any further, but instead turned to gather the team to leave. As I walked away from the eye, a theory began to formulate in my mind. "Perhaps this was not only the oldest petroglyph here, but also one that wasn't carved by any homo sapiens. Could it be the work of the Neanderthals, our predecessors, who preceded us by tens of thousands of years? After all, archeologists have proven by analyzing bones in caves found in Israel that this area was one of the last strongholds of the Neanderthals before going extinct. So, why couldn't it be possible that some of the last Neanderthals, instead of warring with us, shared their most sacred site with early homo sapiens?" It was, of course, only a theory.

I was pondering all this as I called the team on my cellphone, instructing them to regroup for departure. They were scattered across the plateau, each indulging in their own exploration when given the opportunity.

As we all climbed into the helicopter, Eric requested a moment to retrieve his mountain climbing gear from the previous day, including the ropes and pulleys from my rappelling mishap. When he returned, he expressed his gratitude, as this saved him a trek to retrieve it later. As we took off, everyone eagerly discussed their adventures on the plateau. Before landing, Asher mentioned that he needed to return to the mess tent to start dinner. He then turned to me and loudly asked if I had encountered any more snakes on the plateau. I coolly responded, "No, I haven't. Thank God!" I knew he was trying to get a rise out of me, but I didn't give him the satisfaction.

Walking back to our tent to wash up for dinner, Eric inquired if I had found what I was seeking on the plateau. I simply replied yes, without elaborating. My mind was preoccupied with my discoveries and new theories. My vague and distant response piqued his curiosity, but I wasn't ready to divulge more.

That night, we all devoured our dinner, having skipped lunch and subsisting on bottled water and health food snacks during our exploration. The cool, dry desert air had left us famished and exhausted. Personal hygiene was important to me, but with scarce water at our temporary desert camp, our washing and showering facilities were barely adequate. It seemed the situation wouldn't improve until we returned to civilization.

Despite having spent the day with us exploring the ancient art on the plateau, Asher managed to prepare a meal of roasted vegetables, pita bread, pungent but delicious goat cheese, and sweet pudding for dessert. He also found a couple of bottles of Israeli red wine from the Galilee, which I considered the most important items at dinner.

After dinner, I decided to take a walk by myself while Eric and the others caught up on their emails and internet communications. As I strolled around the campsite, I noticed small tents and campsites popping up on the surrounding hilltops. These were tourists who had come to witness the burning bush phenomenon the next day during the winter solstice. Sam and Eric had alerted me to expect an influx of day-tripper tourists tomorrow. The government only allowed them to camp on the surrounding hilltops and not on the floor of the valley where we were. The hilltops, moreover, afforded them an excellent view. However, during the actual midday event, tourists were permitted to also enter the valley floor in front of the burning bush.

As I wandered through our camp, enjoying the calm desert night air, I spotted a group of men sitting around a glowing fire on the valley floor not far from our site. My curiosity piqued, I decided to approach and say hello. As I drew nearer, I counted twelve men, all dressed in white cloth tunics, seated cross-legged, and chanting something in Hebrew that I didn't recognize. I greeted them with "Shalom," and the apparent leader responded in kind. As they all turned to face me, I felt an overwhelming sense of familiarity, even though we'd never met. The leader explained they were Kabbalists, practitioners of the mystical and metaphysical form of Judaism, and here to experience the Lord God's manifestation on earth. Before I could say anything, he continued that they were also here to meet me and deliver a message to me. I was stunned but intrigued too. So I asked if they were certain it was me they wanted to meet. All twelve nodded in affirmation.

Curious, I asked if the twelve of them represented the Twelve Tribes of Israel. Somehow without verbally answering me, I knew it to be true. The leader then conveyed his message to me: "It is time." Confused, I asked, "Time for what?" He replied, "We don't know. That is the only message we have for you. And, one more thing, a warning, beware the Levite Priest!"

Needless to say, I was taken aback. Unsure of how to respond or act, I stepped back from them. They returned their focus to the fire and continued chanting, signaling that our encounter was over. After this I couldn't help but think that this place made everyone a little crazy. It was a good thing we were all leaving the day after tomorrow. As I turned to walk back to our tents, I saw Eric and Asher rushing towards me, concern etched on their faces. I called out, "No need to hurry, I'm fine."

Asher shouted back, "Stay away from those people. They are dangerous." I retorted, "How do you know who they are? These soft-spoken spiritual men are no threat to anyone!" Asher just ignored my question and continued walking towards the twelve Kabbalists. Eric stayed by my side.

As Asher approached the Kabbalists, they began to stand, extinguish their fire, and gather their belongings to leave. Asher loudly warned them that they weren't allowed to camp on the valley floor and should depart immediately. As they turned and walked slowly away, I sensed they were leaving because they had accomplished their purpose—to deliver a message to me—and neither Asher's shouting nor Eric's presence had any impact on them whatsoever.

I watched as Asher positioned himself between me and the departing Kabbalists, ensuring they left the valley floor. I thought to myself, "Who made him camp guardian?" Turning to Eric, who had always been my rock, I linked my arm with his as we slowly walked back to our tent. This gesture was born out of love and a need to be close to him, as well as exhaustion from the day's events.

Since Eric had been helping me learn Hebrew, I asked him about the meaning of Asher's last name, Ben-Levy. He confirmed that, "Ben" meant "son of" in Hebrew, and that Ben-Levy meant "son of Levy." I then inquired if the name Levy had any connection to the ancient Levite priests that Moses had selected as the hereditary priests of the Hebrew people. Eric paused and remarked, "What a strange question," before confirming that names like Levine, Levin, and Levy are descended from the root name Levite. However, he explained that the traditional hereditary designation of who can be a rabbi was no longer followed by modern Jews, except for the very orthodox. Interestingly, he mentioned that while he was on the subject, my last name, "Cohn," was also considered by the orthodox as part of the ancient hereditary priesthood. Everyone else were considered common people. "Why are you interested?" he asked. I replied, "No reason, just curious." But all I could think about was what the Kabbalists had told me.

Upon reaching our tent, we quickly collapsed onto our separate cots, utterly exhausted from the day's physical and emotional challenges in this enigmatic place. Once again, there would be no lovemaking tonight.

CHAPTER 3

THE WINTER SOLSTICE

I slept soundly that night. The next morning, I awoke early, feeling refreshed and ready to start the day. Eric woke up just seconds after me, appearing equally energized. We hugged each other and exchanged a morning kiss. It was the first time since before we married that we had slept in separate beds—or in this case, cots. We were both still adjusting to it. However, we had been so tired at the end of each day here that sleep claimed us the moment our heads touched the pillows. It felt as if a cloud settled over us each night, lulling us to sleep. Meanwhile, I could hear our teammates stirring in their tents. I suggested to Eric that we should hurry to brush our teeth and wash up before the others got to it.

The washing facilities at our desert camp were rudimentary—really just a hose hanging from a pole, connected to a portable water tank. We had to conserve water, so we quickly washed our hands, faces, necks, and brushed our teeth. We just didn't have enough water here for normal showers for this many people in the deep Negev desert. I thought to myself that when we returned to our house in Caesarea, I would spend an entire day luxuriating under a hot shower. The rest of the team soon lined up behind us to wash, as we all began to grow increasingly "ripe."

While we walked to the mess tent, I considered that our efforts would be worthwhile only if we discovered something archeologically significant. However, we hadn't found anything of note yet, and I was unsure what to tell Jacob who was funding the expedition. I even contemplated offering to cover some of the costs myself. It didn't surprise me that he hadn't called me yet. Since Ariel, our talented cameraman and Jacob's son, had likely been providing daily updates. Or, perhaps, Jacob was viewing the uncut uploaded versions of Ariel's filming directly from the cloud. Despite the setbacks, I was not ready to give up yet and remained excited about seeing the burning bush phenomenon that afternoon.

Asher, as usual, had arrived at the mess tent before everyone else and prepared a hearty Israeli breakfast. He typically recited a Hebrew prayer just before the rest of the team arrived, knowing that we all didn't appreciate prolonged prayers.

As we sat down to eat breakfast in the mess tent, a discussion about the winter solstice began. I knew that once Eric started explaining the winter solstice to Ariel and Julie, it would turn into a lecture—to which the entire room listened intently. I thought about how much I had learned from this man. Then an idea hit me. He loved teaching and so he should teach rather than work in the highly dangerous job of a Mossad officer with a cover as a professional archeologist. He could still be an archeologist and do as much extreme sports as he wanted except for one thing—no bullets or knives flying at him! However, I would pick my timing on this needed career change for him. Overcoming my concern, I decided to bury the idea for now. Sam who was sitting across the table from me and also Eric's boss in the Mossad, instantly noticed that I had just thought of something important and just as quickly buried it. Both he and Eric had such finely honed animal instincts for reading people that I had learned to be cautious about revealing my thoughts. I simply told him, "Let's listen to what Eric is saying," which only piqued his curiosity further.

Eric started by explaining that the winter solstice was the longest night of the year but conversely that made the day the shortest day of the year, typically occurring on December 21st on the Gregorian calendar which most of the world uses today. This calendar was established by Pope Gregory XIII in 1582 to standardize calendar dates for Europe. To synchronize the calendar with Earth's rotation around the sun, an extra day is added every four years, called a leap year. This was because the Gregorian calendar lost about six hours every year as related to the earth's rotation around the sun. The extra day during leap year re-synchs the calendar with this rotation. Due to this extra day, the actual winter solstice can occur on December 21st, 22nd, or 23rd. He continued, explaining that the interesting point here was the Jewish calendar is based on moon cycles and doesn't require any corrections, making it more accurate. However, both calendars aligned this year, meaning the pull of the sun on Earth would be at its strongest today compared to the last three years. We were all excited to hear that this would make for the most spectacular burning bush display in the past four years.

I then blurted out loudly that the stars were perfectly aligned for a great show today. Eric turned to me and firmly said that this had nothing to do with any star alignment with Earth, except for the sun. The unspoken part of his statement was, "You haven't listened to a word I said."

Actually, I enjoyed playing the fool occasionally, especially when Eric became too serious and professorial. It lightened the mood. Moreover, I had studied the subtle differences between the Julian, Gregorian, and Lunar calendars at university before Eric was born!

But all I said in response to him was, "Of course you are right. Sometimes you go too fast for me. You are so smart!" This brought an immediate smile to his lips. What can I say but sometimes in relationships, you win by losing. I don't think Ariel and Julie, the newlyweds, or the two young helicopter pilots, understood what had just transpired. But Sam, who had a wife and kids, recognized that I had just scored a point. And Asher, with that smirk on his face—I thought to myself that if only Sam had arrived a minute-and-a-half later the other morning, I would have wiped that smirk off his face. Some people just rubbed me the wrong way.

As we left the mess tent, we saw that the number of day-trip tourists had swollen to at least a hundred. Most were on the hilltops, but some were beginning to make their way down to the valley. From the valley floor, you looked up more than 300 feet to the cave in the mountain where the light show of the burning bush would soon appear. I thought this provided a more authentic perspective of what the ancient Hebrews saw, rather than the view from the surrounding hilltops. I sensed that the tourists hiking down to the valley floor were religious pilgrims, as opposed to the curiosity-seekers on the hilltops. My amazement about this place was confirmed when I saw all the people who still came to witness this phenomenon. After thousands of years the power of this place continued to draw people to worship here.

Sam told the team to hurry to secure a good spot below the cave in the mountain. We all had a head start on everyone, so we managed to get excellent spots up front. We had to wait about an hour for the sun to be in the correct position. During that hour I had a chance to observe our fellow tourists. I saw on their faces the utmost devotion. In other words, I could feel their faith in God. I also spotted the twelve Kabbalists from the previous night, their faces raised and their eyes focused on, from what at this angle, looked like a hole in the mountain. No one spoke to the other but I could hear soft prayers in Hebrew, Arabic, Russian, English, French, and other languages I couldn't recognize fill the air. The people of His Book had gathered from all corners of the earth to praise Him.

As the sun reached its midday zenith, the light show began with just a flicker. Gradually, the light grew stronger and started to bounce off the rocks at the front of the cave. Then, finally, I could see what people have come here for thousands of years to see, the light bounced—actually danced and flickered like a flame off the jagged round rock at the front of the cave entrance. The prayers around me grew louder and I believe I saw some people around me begin to slightly sway as they prayed.

As I witnessed the burning bush phenomenon surrounded by passionate faith in God, I realized this had to be the burning bush of the Exodus. If this was the bush, then this had to be Mount Sinai. But how could I prove it? A hunch came to me as I stood there, knowing that every eye in the valley was focused on the light emanating from the hole. I turned completely around, facing away from the mountain. In other words, I turned my back to God's manifestation on earth. The first thing I saw when I did this were the upturned faces of the faithful. We had arrived early and secured a great viewing position, so I was standing about ten feet higher on the mountain than the group of people below me. I immediately thought that the only other person to do this was Moses when he read the Ten Commandments to the Hebrews. Moses knew that he had to make his commandments stick with his newly adopted people, and what better stage than this light show behind him as he read God's Laws for the first time? It occurred to me that not only was the life of Moses extraordinary but he was also an extraordinarily complex man as well as a master showman.

As I raised my eyes above the heads of the faithful standing or kneeling just below me I saw what Moses would have seen from this spot. The first thing I noticed was the dried-up riverbed and the small hills directly behind it. I couldn't help but especially notice one of the hills because the shadow of the mountain behind me created a shadow in the shape of a triangle or pyramid. The point of the shadow, during the winter solstice, ended directly on one small hill on the other side of the dried-up riverbed.

I recalled reading in the Book of Exodus that when Moses read the Ten Commandments for the first time at the foot of Mount Sinai, he noticed a significant group of Hebrews worshiping a golden calf. He was so incensed that he threw the tablets at it, destroying both the golden calf statue and the tablets. According to Exodus, he then proceeded to pound the golden calf to dust and ordered the deaths of the three thousand idol worshipers. The number three thousand killed was definitely in the Bible. He later carved a second stone tablet with the laws on it. So standing with my back to the burning bush while looking out over the valley at the foot of this mountain, I was trying to determine who Moses really was and what had actually happened here. Was this the real Mount Sinai? At that moment, I was certain that parts of the Exodus story were absolutely true. But I was also sure that later writers had embellished the story to prove a point.

First, Moses was raised as an Egyptian prince. This meant he was literate in an age of illiteracy. He grew up in the Egyptian court, so he had access to all the information brought back by Egyptian emissaries from the surrounding nations. He might have even participated in a few embassy missions himself. Hence, he would have been familiar with the various Semitic tribes inhabiting the Sinai Peninsula before he led the Hebrews through Sinai. He might have also previously visited this burning bush light show as part of one of those Egyptian court missions. So, he probably knew exactly when and where the phenomenon would occur. He also already knew which Semitic tribes he could make deals with and which ones he had to destroy. I also asked myself in what language the original Ten Commandments were written? He could not have written them in hieroglyphics, the language of their hated former Egyptian masters. The ancient Hebrews spoke Proto-Hebrew (also called Paleo-Hebrew), a Semitic language similar to ancient Canaanite or Phoenician, but did not have a written language yet. I believe the Bible was correct when it stated that it took Moses (the Hand of God) a long time to write the Ten Commandments. The Bible said it took forty days and nights to write them, and it was during this time that dissent developed in the Hebrew camp. I also believe Moses took some Egyptian court acolytes and scribes with him when he left—scribes who also believed in the One God and who knew many of the ancient Middle Eastern dialects and languages. I believe that he actually gave the ancient Hebrews a written language at Mount Sinai, which archeologists now call Proto-Hebrew. And this was the language in which the Ten Commandments were first written. This, of course, is just a hunch. We also know today that it was several hundred years after this Sinai event that the oral histories of the Hebrews were first codified into the Bible.

Next, as I tried to get into the mind of a man who had been dead for more than three thousand years, I realized that when he looked out from this spot, he must have seen a flowing river, not the dried-up riverbed that it is now. Moreover, the ancient Egyptians believed that one side of the Nile River was the land of the living, and the other side was the land of the dead. This structure of the world in his mind would have been difficult for him to reject, even if he now believed in one God versus many. Perhaps Moses looked out from where I was standing and saw a lush, flowing river that reminded him of the Nile River. Maybe the shadow of this mountain was pointing to something that Moses still thought of as being in the Land of the Dead—across on the other side of the river. In Egypt, the Land of the Dead is where all the tombs were located!

All these thoughts went through my mind in a matter of moments. The burning bush phenomenon was still going strong, and the whole team remained transfixed by its light show. I realized that it would not last much longer, so I quickly started walking towards where the tip of the shadow on the other side of the ancient riverbed was pointing while at the height of the burning bush phenomenon. My other team members were looking up, captivated by this rare spectacle of light. They did not notice me leave, and I didn't have time to stop and explain.

As I walked forward towards the shadow's endpoint beyond the group of pilgrims, I realized that if I was going on such a hike, I might need my utility belt back in my tent. On it hung my water canteen, flashlight, and hunting knife. I would also need my brown fedora hat. My cellphone was already in my pocket. I had learned through experience that all of these items were absolutely necessary, even vital for deep desert hikes. I ran back to my tent, picked up my utility belt, and ran back to the shadow of Mount Karkom, attaching the utility belt around my waist as I did so. I was almost out of breath but excited and fixated on my new observation. I could see that the shadow had already begun to move and change, but it was still close enough to the original hill for me to get my bearings. As I approached my destination—the tip of the shadow from Mount Karkom—all my movements slowed. I had to check every couple of minutes by looking back to ensure I was constantly walking in a straight line from the now-fading burning bush light show. As I was walking across the dry riverbed, I looked down and noticed how smooth the rocks were. I thought to myself that only thousands of years of running water could make them this smooth. The unevenness and smoothness of the river rocks further slowed me down. I did not want to stumble and fall while looking ahead and keeping track of what was behind me.

I finally reached the other side of the dry river. That's when I noticed that the burning bush light show had stopped. And now, what seemed at a distance to be relatively small and smooth rocks had started getting bigger. The rocks on the edge of the river came up to my knees, while the further away from the river's edge, the bigger they became—finally qualifying as huge boulders. Behind those were several hills and then came the high ridges where most of the day-tripper tourists were located.

Even though I had been careful to keep my bearings as I tried to walk a straight path to the point of the shadow from the top of Mount Karkom, I now realized I was getting confused about which small hill—or up close, much bigger, more like a small mountain—the shadow was pointing to. It took me about two hours to get to this point and I knew I didn't have much sunlight left since the winter solstice is the shortest day of the year. I had to double up my search efforts while the images were still fresh in my mind.

Then my cellphone started ringing. It was Eric calling. I knew that I would have to stop and explain myself. On the other hand, it felt good to have someone who cared about where the heck I was. So when I answered the call, I thought, "Boy, can he yell!" He had been looking all over the place for me and had seen that my utility belt had also gone. I let him get it all out of his system. I could tell he was very worried and very angry that I had disappeared.

In response, I apologized for disappearing and worrying him and the team. I told him that I was fine but had a new idea and the short time of the shadow on which it was based meant I had to act very quickly to follow it up. I had no time to explain myself. I also said that I didn't want to disturb his enjoyment of the burning bush phenomenon. Additionally, I told him that I was among the rocks on the other side of the dry riverbed, somewhere in front of the burning bush hole in the mountain. I explained that I needed more time to explore this area, and that I loved him and not to worry; I would be back later. I didn't have any more time to explain because the sun was starting to set and I needed the daylight to find what I was looking for. I told him I loved him again and hung up. I didn't know it at the time, but as soon as I hung up, he began organizing a rescue party to find me.

His phone call had really disoriented me as to where the small mountain was located that the shadow had been pointing. I began to walk back to the edge of the dry river so I could reorient myself by getting a clearer view of the area—not so blocked by all these boulders.

As I retraced my steps, I tried to focus and remember the exact direction of the shadow. As I reached the far edge of the dry riverbed, I looked again at the now dark hole in Mount Karkom. I also surveyed the tops of the surrounding area and noticed that all the day trippers on the ridges and religious pilgrims on the valley floor had departed. All were gone, but strangely, I didn't feel alone.

Then it happened. As the sun was setting, the dark hole in the mountain came alive again. But this time, the sun streaming through the hole wasn't in the shape of a burning bush; it had transformed the rock shape of the hole into an eye. It was the same Eye of God etched in stone on the plateau on top of Mount Karkom that I had seen earlier—an image with such strange power that I had backed away from it. This realization both thrilled and terrified me at the same time. And the light streaming from this one eye came straight over my right shoulder and made a direct hit on a small mountain. I knew instantly that it was the same mountain that the shadow had pointed to earlier! Bingo! Found it! But it was getting darker now, so I took out my flashlight from my holster and turned it on.

As I turned again to make sure I was following the streaming ray of light to the correct mountain, my foot accidentally got caught in a crevice between the rocks, and I sprained my ankle. It hurt like hell, and I fell hard against the rock that had caught my foot. I braced my fall with my two outstretched hands, one of them holding my flashlight. I heard the crack of my flashlight hit the rock but luckily brace my fall. When I got up from this, my flashlight began to flicker and then went off. Frustrated, I said out loud, "God damn it!" Raised my right hand holding the now useless flashlight above me and threw it down, striking the rock with it. As it struck the rock it burst into a hundred pieces.

When this happened, something deep inside me made me realize that I had just cursed in front of the Eye of God while He was looking directly at me. I then did something I had never done before because I don't even pray. I turned and looked directly at the light in the mountain and said out loud, "Please God, forgive me for taking your name in vain." And the strangest thing of all was that I genuinely meant it.

Seconds later, the light in the hole of Mount Karkom went out. The sun had set, and when the sun sets in the desert before the stars and moon come out, it is a time of complete and utter blackness. So there I was, with a bad ankle caught in a rock crevice in the middle of nowhere in the deep Negev desert, and it was so dark that I literally couldn't see my hand in front of my face.

MEMORIES OF TIMES LOST

So I tried to make myself comfortable by sitting on one of the rocks where my foot was caught. I needed some time to strategize an escape from this predicament. I attempted to slightly move my foot and pull it free but to no avail. I was stuck. Then, the idea of untying my boot laces crossed my mind. But before I could act, I noticed a series of lights bouncing back and forth, moving towards me. They resembled a bobbing necklace of diamonds set against the black velvet night. A beautiful sight, but how embarrassing—it was clear that my teammates were coming to rescue me!

I hadn't called Eric to explain the situation and ask for his help, because it meant I had to be rescued again! I would have preferred to walk back to camp guided by my cellphone flashlight, but I was too stuck. So instead, I used my phone light as a beacon to guide them directly to me. Funny thing was that they were already heading directly at me even without the light from my cellphone.

I waited for them to get close before I casually started speaking. I never uttered the word "Help!" Although I was thinking it, I was trying to maintain some dignity.

Soon, they were all here—Eric, Sam, Ariel (with his camera filming), Julie, and even the two young helicopter pilots. They had all come to find me. The only one absent was Asher which I duly noted but said nothing.

However, I realized I had to talk fast to make this look more like an impromptu outdoor team meeting rather than a rescue mission. So I began by commenting that it was a beautiful night for a walk in the desert. And by the way, I had some good news and bad news to discuss with them. I suggested everyone take a seat on the rocks and relax. Their faces betrayed their concern, curiosity and confusion, and I could tell Eric was miffed. But despite their skepticism I plowed on.

First, I mentioned that the good news was that I found the site we needed to explore. It was behind me in the hills. That means we wouldn't be breaking camp tomorrow but would continue here for at least one more day. At this point, Sam asked if I was certain about the potential of the site. I responded confidently, though Eric's penetrating gaze demanded more explanation. However, I held my tongue about the mysterious Kabbalists or the fact that I felt it was God himself who showed me the way.

So I sidestepped the problem by answering him in my most scientifically, cold, and logical way. I explained to him about the shadow I saw as I looked out from Mount Karkom during the winter solstice that pointed to a specific mountain on this side of the dry river bed close to where we now sit. Also, I told them all about the one-eyed stone petroglyph on the plateau on top of Karkom and how its image matched the second stream of light which pointed me to the same small mountain. I intentionally did not mention the power I felt emanated from this carving of the one eye or the message the Kabbalists gave me. I also explained my theory that, when Moses looked out from the foot of Mount Karkom and saw this same river bed where we were sitting so near, that it possibly reminded him of the Nile River. If so, it also reminded him that the Nile River divided Egypt into the Land of the Living and the Land of the Dead. And we were sitting now on the side of the ancient dry river bed that Moses would consider the Land of the Dead. And lastly, (this is when Eric blinked) all the Egyptian tombs are located in the Land of the Dead. When I mentioned the word "tomb" their eyes widened and bodies stiffened in the dim flashlight glow.

Turning to Sam, I said that if he brought his stone-penetrating equipment tomorrow, we could determine if the mountain had a hollow space in less than three hours. I would call Jacob after we did that tomorrow to update him.

"In the meantime, I just want to let you all know the bad news about my minor mishap. My foot is caught in this crevice and I can't get it out." I then continued that I was about to untie the laces and slip my foot out before they arrived. Julie immediately jumped up and said to me, "Don't you dare. If your ankle has swollen you will never get your boot back on it and we have a bit of a walk back to camp." She then asked Eric and Sam both to help. Sam grabbed both sides of my boot and pulled while Eric lifted me straight up. My boot gave way instantly under their efforts and I was free! Julie checked my ankle and diagnosed it as likely sprained, suggesting Tylenol tablets and a good night's sleep was all I needed. As I stood up Eric put his arm around my waist to support me so I could put most of my weight off my injured foot.

Before starting the walk back, I asked Sam to mark a rock about twenty feet away with my fedora hat by tucking it into the earth in front of it. I explained it was the small mountain where we were going to explore tomorrow morning. Sam said he would do it but also attach a digital tracker to the rock. "Much like the tracker we put on your phone before arriving here," he added nonchalantly. "How do you think we found you so fast? We always knew where you were." I was too tired to comment, but I just shook my head and thought to myself, "Well, that's the good news and bad news of being married to a Mossad officer." However, I made a mental note to discuss with Eric this tracker that was put on my phone without my permission another time when I was in better shape.

I limped slowly back as we both held onto each other. The team soon left us behind but I didn't mind. I was with my partner and that was what mattered to me. And I could tell he was responding. His support felt more than just a safety measure. I hoped that tonight we might finally make love again.

Upon returning to our tent, Julie, Ariel, and Sam were waiting. Removing my boot hurt like hell and I apologized for the smell emanating from my socks, which was met with laughter. I joked that Ariel should film in Paris next, so we could all stay in fabulous hotels and smell of expensive French cologne. They all laughed again. I also appreciated Julie's commitment to Ariel, despite his father's money, and despite the dust, sweat, and danger, I decided that she was not only beautiful but also tough as nails and a real asset to our expedition.

Eric had briefly disappeared from our tent and reappeared holding two plates of roasted chicken and pita bread and a bottle of wine peeking out from his army jacket pocket. As everyone began leaving, Julie handed me a bottle of water and instructed me to drink it. Eric and I were finally alone. I gulped down the water, not realizing how thirsty I was—more thirsty than hungry.

After a couple of bites of chicken and some pita bread, I told Eric that I needed to rest. The day's exertion had gotten to me. He immediately stopped eating too and lay down beside me on my cot, supporting me as I drifted off. Eric always knew when I had reached my limit. That night, I fell asleep in the arms of my ruggedly handsome blond partner. But there was no lovemaking again; we seemed to be turning into a pair of celibate monks.

Every night since we arrived in this strangely mysterious and sacred valley in front of Mount Karkom, I had slept like a rock. But this night I had the strangest dream which was so vivid, I remembered every detail even when I woke the next day. Again, I felt the power of this place pull me into a dreamlike, surreal space where the boundary between reality and the mystical disappeared.

In my dream I was walking—gliding, actually—down the middle of a huge room. It seemed like it was a throne room in an ancient Egyptian palace. It had seven towering pillars on either side, holding up a very high roof above me. The pillars were covered in hieroglyphics carved into the stone. But instead of the usual familiar pale, weathered colors that archeologists associated with them, the pillars were sheathed in pure shimmering gold hammered onto the stone reliefs stretching up as high as the eye could see. Next, I noticed the room was filled with a pink haze in the air which smelled slightly of burnt cinnamon and myrrh. It was a faintly sweet delicate aroma. It looked and smelled so familiar but that was impossible because I had never been to such a place. I also immediately recognized it as the fragrant incense used by the royal court of ancient Egypt. It reminded me of home, yet, I thought, "How could that be?" I also faintly saw out of the corner of my eye the nobles of Egyptian court staring at me as I passed them. None of them spoke. But I also knew that I knew them all. I sensed they were shocked to see me. They were dressed in robes of the finest white linen, adorned with jewelry of turquoise, gold, lapis lazuli, amethyst and carnelian. Behind them were slaves fanning the whole place with fans made of peacock and ostrich feathers which circulated a delightful breeze in the room. I was also aware that the perfume they were using smelled of frankincense, lemongrass, and roses. Again, in my dream, it was such a familiar scent to me. It was the scent of home! Impossible I know. My brain, moreover, was telling me that no one had smelled these perfumes in more than three thousand years.

Finally, in my dream, I as was gliding closer to the end of the hall where the Pharaoh was seated looking directly at me. He was dressed in all-gold garments and sat on a golden throne atop seven granite steps, each step representing a level of the Egyptian afterlife with the Pharaoh as a living god sitting on top of it all. The sun shone on him threw the high up square-cut windows in the stone walls of the palace and it made him glitter as I approached. He was wearing the crown of upper and lower Egypt and held his solid gold scepter in the shape of a question mark encrusted with precious stones that signified the unification of Egypt and conquest of Nubia. He was without a doubt the absolute ruler of the strongest military power in the world. All this I knew was meant to impress the common people and visiting foreign diplomats but somehow it didn't impress me.

In my dream I already knew them all including this boy Pharaoh Tutankhamun, my former student when I was chief priest to his father, the Pharaoh Amenhotep IV. I had helped his father close all the pagan temples and tried to turn Egypt towards the worship of the one true God. But, while I was away on a diplomatic mission to Canaan, my Pharaoh, who was also my friend, had died.

In my dream, as I approached the platform where the new Pharaoh was seated, I couldn't help but notice how different everything felt. I was accustomed to standing on that platform at the Pharaoh's right side; now, I stood on the ground below, looking up. I've studied the characters of ancient Egyptian archeology extensively, but to see them all so vividly alive in my dream was both unsettling and captivating.

First, I noticed Ay standing behind the Pharaoh. Much loved by the people, Ay now held the title of Grand Vizier, but was too old and feeble to be anything but a buffer between the new Pharaoh and the real power here, General Horemheb. The general was the Commander in Chief of the army and chariot corps and in my absence, had allied himself with the priests of Amun-Re to restore all the old pagan gods. He had black eyes that held the cold glint of a serpent, and he now stood on the steps half way to the top of the royal throne platform, closer to power than ever before. And indeed, I knew him to be a slithering serpent. Now in my dream we locked eyes. He immediately lowered his eyes. He never could look directly at me because he knew I saw him for what he truly was.

I also knew that he had systematically slaughtered all the priests of the One True God except for the ones that I had managed to save. These survivors took refuge with my Hebrew tribe. He didn't dare attack the Hebrews yet. The new Pharaoh, Tutankhamun, would not permit it. But one burning question lingered in my mind: How long can this fragile boy-king live? Also, through the haze of my dream I noticed an elderly woman on the royal platform dressed all in silver and looking so sad. I felt a son's love for his mother upon seeing her but could not be sure of her identity.

Looking up as I stood on the floor below the royal platform, I saw the Pharaoh start to rise from his throne to address me. He rose slowly and used a wooden cane sheathed in gold to steady himself. I had to restrain myself from running up the stone steps to help him, as I had done countless times before, but today was different. I knew that if I dared touch the stone steps even with the hem of my garment, I would be cut in half by the royal guards lurking in the shadows protecting the king. However, we both knew he could not walk to the platform's edge to speak to me because his club foot caused him too much pain.

To my surprise, he began to shout at me, his words echoing through the palace in ancient Egyptian, a language unheard for over three millennia. Yet it was familiar to me. I understood him perfectly. He was cursing me, demanding that I leave Egypt immediately with the damn Hebrews and take as much gold as we could carry. That was what I, along with the whole court, had heard. But his eyes looking directly at me told me something else. The eyes of this gentle boy told me he could not hold General Horemheb back much longer. We both knew this, and more importantly, they spoke of his secret: That he still was a true believer in the One True God!

Then, he did something completely unexpected. He raised his hand above his head and threw his scepter at me. Initially, I thought he was attempting to strike me but I quickly realized he was trying to give it to me. Lacking the strength to throw it all the way, the scepter clattered down the unforgiving granite steps, landing in front of me. As I bent to retrieve it, I marveled at its weight, heavy with gold and covered in jewels. But I also observed at the same moment that the fall on the granite steps had dented it in the middle of its handle where it had struck the steps.

As I stood up holding the dented scepter, my dream completely dissolved and changed. Suddenly, I was riding in a cart amidst a desert. The court's perfumed aroma transformed into the stink of human and horse sweat mingled with intense desert heat. I also noticed the people around me were dressed in rough leather garments—really more akin to animal skins than leather. Huge clouds of dust stirred by the moving flocks of goats and sheep made it difficult to breathe. And there must have been thousands of people all marching in the same direction, under the relentless, blistering heat of the sun and choking dust.

I felt it was so beastly hot as I surveyed my surroundings. My gaze was immediately drawn to dozens of ox-drawn carts. Suddenly, I found myself standing by one, lifting its hide skin cover to reveal the cargo. A sight both astounding and terrifying met my eyes—it was the treasure of Egypt. The Pharaoh had said to take it and we had obliged. The carts were laden with heaps of gold and silver. The sight was alarming because I knew that while General Horemheb might allow the slaves to leave the country, especially to avoid a major slave rebellion and civil war, he would never let this much treasure permanently leave Egypt. I knew immediately that this treasure was a problem and was slowing us down. And that he would come to bring it back murdering all of us at the same time. As soon as possible we had to reach terrain, such as the wilderness, where chariots could not follow. But neither could these slow-moving, heavy, ox-pulled carts laden with gold! I realized this was a problem. I also knew that luckily for us the Game of Thrones-style palace political intrigue back in Egypt should slow Horemheb down at least for a while.

Now in my dream, I was walking along with my people and suddenly several men rushed towards me, shouting in a language I didn't recognize but inexplicably understood. It must have been Proto-Hebrew—the language of the slaves. I then looked ahead to see at what they were pointing. I instantly recognized the plateau of Mount Karkom. However, they were not yelling "Mount Karkom" but "Mount Sinai! Mount Sinai! Mount Sinai!" In my dreamlike state of mind, I absolutely knew we had reached God's Mountain. Karkom was Sinai!

Just then, I was rudely awakened from my dream and sleep by Ariel. He came running up to our tent, pulled back the canvas entrance flap, stuck his head inside and shouted that we should both wake up and come quick to see what was happening outside. It was nothing less than a miracle!

CHAPTER 5

·～ৡৡﾟ·

DANCING UNDER DINOSAURS

Late last summer, months before arriving at our current dig site, Eric and I were driving back home in his old, reliable Jeep. We were coming from Jacob Kurtz's celebration party honoring our major archeological discovery of King Herod's royal jewels. I was exhausted from our day exploring Caesarea and then attending the party. But, at the same time, so excited that Eric and I had just decided to get married that my brain was spinning. The journey back to our small rental apartment in Jerusalem whizzed by so quickly, I hardly noticed the time it took to get home. I couldn't even recall who proposed to whom first. But that didn't matter. All I do remember is that we both said, "Yes!" The only phrase that kept repeating in my head was the old Barbra Streisand song, "Sadie, Sadie, married lady." And that was going to be me—a Sadie—a married lady! Eric didn't say much during the drive, but he sported a big smile the whole way home. It felt he was actually beaming at me.

When we arrived home, we were both so spent that we promptly fell asleep in each other's arms. Come morning, Eric rose early for his daily run and workout. When he returned, we both showered together, then proceeded to make love for nearly three hours—a personal record. We were insatiable. I was starting to understand my soon-to-be life partner's biorhythms. The best times for us to make love were after he worked out and showered or when we found ourselves in unusual or risky locations. This time we showered again, then realized that we were both starving. We walked over to a small nearby restaurant and ate so much that the proprietor began giving us odd looks. By the time we finished eating, the organized, pragmatic and business-like parts of my brain took control again. We had to plan our next archeological expedition before the deadline of the next winter solstice on December 21, not to mention our wedding and honeymoon. Moreover, I had also just remembered that I arranged a meeting with our team at Solomon Levine's office, our lawyer, in town that day at 4PM to discuss the legal and logistical aspects of our next expedition. I now realized I had to focus!

Again, even though I knew the expedition's real deadline—being on site in the Negev at Mount Karkom before December 21 to observe the winter solstice—I first needed to start discussing our wedding and honeymoon plans. I had to nail it or I wouldn't be able to concentrate on anything else.

Eric, as always, was ambivalent about the details of the wedding and honeymoon. That meant that I had to make the decisions about such things as usual. In the meantime, we relaxed at the apartment until it was time to leave for the meeting. It seemed like we both had permanent smiles on our faces all afternoon including when we arrived at Solomon's office. The team was all there and consisted of Sam Reichman, Ariel Kurtz, Solomon Levine, Eric Jansen, and myself, Mark Cohn. Everyone was seated at the conference table. Jacob Kurtz also joined via a Zoom call on Solomon's computer. It took all my mental strength not to start the meeting by discussing our upcoming wedding and possible honeymoon destinations.

Collecting myself, I began by reiterating why I had called it. I proceeded to review my observation from my trip to Mount Karkom with Eric: While standing on the ridge of the mountain's plateau, I had seen below, what looked like very specific edges of an ancient road ending abruptly at the side of the mountain. My strong hunch was that there must be a hidden cave inside the mountain, possibly containing artifacts that could give us archeological proof that the

Exodus was real and that Mount Karkom was actually the biblical Mount Sinai. I also expressed my gratitude to Jacob for agreeing to fund a second expedition and hoped he still felt the same way today. Although I had explained this at the previous night's party, when I did it now it all seemed much more real in the cold light of day with no alcohol to make everyone more agreeable. Everyone listened intently. Sam spoke first, congratulating Eric and me on our engagement and also Ariel on his. He gave us a joyful "Mazel Tov!" but quickly refocused on the meeting's purpose. He pointed out that due to the new expedition's location, it would be considerably more expensive. We had to consider the logistics of camping in the Negev as well as transportation there and back. He continued that we had been somewhat spoiled because our last dig site was so close to Jerusalem that we all could go home each night for a good meal and sleep in our own beds. This wouldn't be the case in the remote desert wilderness of the Negev!

However, Sam suggested a possible solution, despite acknowledging that the expedition would be more expensive, uncomfortable, and dangerous than our last, with no guarantee of finding anything.

As Sam spoke, I also remembered that he had previously guessed my real reason for pushing this expedition now.

It was to keep Eric safe from as many dangerous Mossad assignments as possible. I figured it was better for him to be sweating next to me in the desert, doing something he loved where I could keep an eye on him rather than risking his life on some dangerous spy mission. Nor would I ever reveal my true intentions to Eric and would deny it if Sam brought it up. I would be afraid that Eric would be furious at me. So as Sam spoke, I remained silent. Nothing I heard him say so far deterred me from this desert expedition.

Sam continued, stating that he would be in charge of the radar equipment again, which would help us locate anything hidden inside the mountain or underground. Since he didn't know what was going to be needed, he would have to transport all the newest LIDAR and GPR equipment as well as the latest laser equipment. Unlike the last dig, if he needed a part, he could not just take a short ride over to his company's warehouse to pick it up. Ariel interjected at this point, mentioning that he too would have to figure out how to transport all his film and video equipment. Then Jacob interrupted to ask Sam a question. He said he understood the logistics and expenses of a desert archeological expedition. This wasn't Israel's first. But before we delved further into potential logistical problems, he wanted Sam to explain his proposed solution.

We all turned to Sam who took a deep breath and looked straight at me. He revealed that because I had the audacity or sheer dumb luck to ask the Israeli Prime Minister at Jacob's party to authorize this Negev expedition to Mount Karkom, including the same previous teammates and because we were so successful in finding the royal jewels of King Herod on our last archeological dig, the Prime Minister gave his permission. The PM had also assigned both Eric and him to the project. Sam continued that he believed the reason for their unusual assignment to this archeological expedition (besides my request) was twofold. First, the site was very close, possibly too close, to the sensitive Egyptian border and he didn't want any unwanted incidents. Second, the site was still considered sacred by many, and he didn't want any of us, but especially me, trampling over any holy spots or relics. Moreover, the PM further said that he was going to make sure that this permission would allow us to use the facilities at the Israeli military training reserve located close to Mount Karkom. Hence, this expedition would be considered a quasi-military expedition. It was the only way we had received permission to proceed. Furthermore, the PM said he would explore the possibility of the expedition striking a deal to use military helicopters for transportation. Sam continued that not only was this site where we wanted to explore and possibly dig still considered sacred by many people, but it also has been designated as a UNESCO World Heritage site, an Israeli national park, and a restricted military training area. He then jokingly added that the only site more difficult to explore and dig up would be the Temple Mount itself! He emphasized that getting the Prime Minister's permission was crucial to this expedition—and I had secured it!

In response I could not help a half-smile, as I addressed the team, but my gaze was fixed on Jacob's face on the computer. I had a quick anecdote to share and it went something like this: "Suppose you're strolling alone on a beach and you stumble upon an old copper lamp. When you rub it, a genie appears and grants you only one wish. What would you wish for? Most people might wish for either health, wealth, or love, but I would wish for luck. Consider this: luck covers everything."

Still speaking directly to Jacob, I continued, "Perhaps it was dumb luck that we found all that treasure on our previous expedition. However, I will take any kind of luck I can get. Besides, wouldn't you rather invest in someone who was lucky at finding stuff? The discovery of King Tut's tomb in Egypt was, after all, a result of sheer dumb luck."

The whole table was dead silent after I told this story. A long minute passed before Jacob burst into laughter, agreeing wholeheartedly with my perspective. However, he was still curious about the final deal that Sam and Eric could negotiate with their military contacts but, in the meantime, offered me the same arrangement as last time: $20 million for all media and promotional rights to whatever we might find. Acknowledging the greater costs of this expedition over the last one, he offered an advance of $2 million for initial expenses, to be subtracted from the $20 million. The balance would be divided among the team members like the last time or with any adjustments as I thought appropriate. However, should we fail to find anything within thirty days from the first time we arrive on the mountain (the start date to be agreed upon later), then the deal was terminated and I would owe him one million dollars for upfront costs. Essentially, if we found nothing, we'd share the burden of the upfront costs. After a brief pause, I negotiated the terms to sixty days. Jacob took a moment to think about it and agreed. Then I turned to Solomon, our attorney, and asked him to please draw up the contract.

As Jacob was about to end his call, he quickly added one last comment which was that both Ariel and Solomon had something to discuss with Eric and me before, in his usual style, abruptly disconnecting. Sam, taking this as his cue to exit the meeting, asked Eric to meet him the next morning to start coordinating the logistics of our archeological dig in the Negev with the various Israeli departments, especially the military. Eric agreed to the meeting without hesitation.

After Sam departed the meeting, Eric, Ariel, Solomon and I were alone sitting at Solomon's conference room table. So I asked Ariel, "What's up?" Ariel responded with a half-smile, "Remember at Jacob's party, when I told you I'd get my father to give you a great price on the house you both liked? The ultra-modern one near the bottom of the hill, close to him, the one he lived in before building his new Roman-style villa at the top of the hill?" He continued, "Well, since Julie and I agreed that we don't want to live there—nothing wrong with the house, mind you—we just don't want to live that close to Jacob. So, I convinced him to sell it to you at a fantastic price." Ariel explained that he also wanted to thank me for believing in him, basically launching his career as a photographer/filmmaker, and making him financially independent. He then revealed that Jacob's asking price for the house was 14 million shekels. Rapidly calculating, I realized it was approximately 3.5 million dollars at a conversion rate of four shekels to the dollar. According to Ariel, this price equaled the cost to build the property, including the land, years ago and was well below current market value. Lastly, Ariel added that this price could be considered a wedding present to us from the Kurtz family.

I turned to Eric and asked if he still wanted to live there. He responded that he sure did but asked if we could afford it. I assured him we could. Addressing Ariel and Solomon, I exclaimed, "Yes!" I added that I wanted the house purchased in both Eric's name and mine and that we wanted to pay for it in cash. Solomon agreed but mentioned that after our marriage, he'd adjust the house's ownership status to reflect us as a married couple for tax purposes. I asked how soon we could move in given the house was currently unoccupied. Solomon assured us it would take just a couple of days since we were paying in full. He just needed to complete the paperwork and collect signatures. Ariel chimed in, stating Jacob was selling the house "as is" including the custom furniture but not the art, and that the property had been well maintained. I responded swiftly that I saw no need for a second house tour, expressing a desire to move quickly for fear that Jacob might change his mind.

Turning to Eric, I tried to gauge his feelings about the agreement. Sensing his unease at the rapid pace of the transaction, I attempted to soothe him by noting we'd soon have a home of our own. I also teased him about having to replace all his sporting equipment that his former girl friend,

Julie had discarded after their break-up. I couldn't help but chuckle at the mental image of her throwing out his snow skis, diving gear, skydiving parachute, mountain climbing equipment, and more. My chuckling was infectious, causing everyone, including Eric, to join in. His laughter reassured me that he was on board with the house purchase. I added that while he was shopping for new sports equipment, I would be buying art for our new house. I do indeed love buying art! Moreover, I added that I would only buy Israeli artists for our new home.

Shifting gears, I thanked Ariel for his help on this and asked about his wedding and honeymoon plans with Julie. He shared their idea of a small wedding in Israel at Jacob's house in Caesarea and a grand reception in New York City. The honeymoon destination was yet undecided, but they were considering sailing around the Greek Isles. He then turned the question back to us about our plans.

Eric responded that we hadn't really discussed it yet. He was aware that Israel recognized gay marriage from other countries but it did not allow it to be performed legally within its borders. So, we would have to get married abroad. He added that we would definitely keep everyone informed about our decision. I was relieved to hear Eric's thoughts on the matter.

Unexpectedly, he then asked Ariel what they would like for a wedding gift from us. Ariel pondered for a second before his face lit up. He admitted he'd never been skydiving. Eric promptly offered to "take him up" and dive with him, extending the invitation to Julie as well. However, he didn't think she would do it. Ariel said he would ask her but also doubted she'd agree.

When Ariel asked when they could go, Eric replied that he had a meeting with Sam the next day but they could do it the day after. He asked Ariel to meet him early in a private airport on the edge of the northern part of the Negev near Be'er Sheva (Beersheba) at 6AM. Eric explained he'd teach Ariel to pack his parachute first, then they would jump. The whole day would be on him. The pilot and skydiving instructor were army friends of his. An overwhelming feeling of anxiety washed over me. The idea of an "out of the blue" situation that put my partner in danger as well as a good friend and that I could not control was terrifying. The meeting adjourned shortly after. I told Eric that I needed a drink. He agreed. I knew I had to play this situation smartly so as not to look like a scared old man. I knew I was absolutely against it but had to find a creative way to manage it.

We found a hole-in-the-wall wine bar near Solomon's Jerusalem office and settled in to enjoy some wine. There, Eric mentioned that tomorrow he wanted to check with Sam first before he agreed to any travel time out of the country for our wedding and get the parameters of this new archeological expedition with Sam before agreeing to anything. The way he said this made me think he was cautious about possible ulterior motives from Mossad. But I said nothing except to be sure to invite both Sam and Alisa, his wife, to our wedding.

As we enjoyed some wine and a light dinner, I felt it was a good time (if there was such a thing) to bring up the subject of the sky dive he and Ariel were planning the day after tomorrow. Trying to appear casual, I asked Eric if it wasn't too risky to take an inexperienced person like Ariel up 20,000 feet(6096m) and jump out of a perfectly good plane. Eric reassured me that they'd only be jumping from 11,000 feet(3353m). As if the difference in altitude made any difference to me! When he said this I could not help but think to myself it doesn't matter—any height seemed too fucking dangerous!

Eric then surprised me by revealing something about himself I had not known: that before he joined Mossad, he was part of the Sayeret Matkal, the Special Forces of Israel equivalent to the US Navy Seals where he had jumped from planes dozens of times. He explained that the thrill of it was fun and not at all dangerous when you knew what you were doing. He further reassured me that there was also a strong possibility that Ariel might be too scared to jump, in which case Eric would jump solo. Or maybe Ariel will want to jump the first time "in tandem" with the instructor. That was when the first timer is tied to the front of the instructor and they jump together while the instructor controls everything. He then continued that he was beginning to know me very well and I did not have to say a word for him to know when I was nervous and disagreed with him. I now realized his decision was final. So, reluctantly, I asked him if it would be alright if I could come to the airfield to watch him jump. He agreed, suggesting it would be fun for me to watch and even take some photos.

Leaving the restaurant, it occurred to me that I had intended to manage him, but he had managed me instead. Isn't that what marriage is all about? Regardless, if something went wrong, I wanted to be there to pick up the pieces and not hear about it over the phone. I thought to myself, "Some fun, eh?" We then proceeded to slowly drive back to our small rental apartment and fall asleep in each other's arms. But before we fell asleep, I tried to be optimistic and relaxed when I told Eric to take a good look at this place because our new home is going to be a drastic change for the better! However, I could nor shake my feeling of danger.

The next morning Eric left our place very early to meet Sam and negotiate with several Israeli departments including the military. We would need not only their permission but also their cooperation to ensure the success of our upcoming archeological expedition.

I spent the day exploring art galleries in Jerusalem, each displaying a unique blend of art and archeology. Original artifacts and copies were scattered around, challenging visitors to discern between the two. Despite the intellectual challenge, my mind was elsewhere and I didn't end up buying anything. Time flew by and, before I knew it, I was joining Eric for a cocktail at the rooftop bar of the Mamilla Hotel. But even there, I couldn't shake off my anxiety over his skydive the following day.

Eric, always focused on the task at hand, wanted to discuss the progress he and Sam had made getting everything lined up for our upcoming archeological expedition to the Negev. It seemed that everything was proceeding smoothly, including the provision of two helicopters. Their crews had even volunteered to help set up our camp. Everyone in Israel appeared to be an amateur archeologist! But I found myself barely listening, the impending skydive dominating my thoughts.

We decided to stay at the hotel for dinner as well. During our meal, Eric mentioned that he thought it would be good idea to go to Egypt for our honeymoon, where he could serve as my guide due to his fluency in Arabic and skill in deciphering hieroglyphics. He had been there many times and would enjoy visiting again. Enthusiastically, I agreed, admitting I had never been to Egypt and looked forward to the adventure.

Since we were on the subject of our honeymoon, I took the opportunity to bring up the subject of our wedding. My suggestion was to get a marriage license and hold the ceremony in New York City, officiated by a rabbi. This would also give me a chance to introduce Eric to my relatives living in the area. Additionally, we could fly in Eric's relatives from abroad — his mother, his brother and his wife, and maybe his father who lives in Holland. I was sure they would all like to see New York City and would even consider it a mini vacation. Naturally, we would pay for everything. Also, it didn't hurt that, as a native New Yorker, I could be the guide and speak the local language—it's a form of English. He laughed at my small joke and agreed with everything except he did not want to invite his father. Eric explained that his father had abandoned his family when he was three and his brother was seven years old and he had never forgiven his father. His father had not spoken to him or his family since then and Eric saw no reason at all why he should attend the wedding. I immediately agreed but also thought to myself that Eric was finally opening up to me about himself.

We continued to discuss our plans, aiming to align our wedding with Ariel and Julie's reception to avoid unnecessary travel. We'd invite them to our ceremony, of course, since we were attending theirs in Israel. But, to ensure all these plans would work, we would need to coordinate the logistics closely. One fixed point was that we all had to be back in time for the winter equinox at Mount Karkom.

After dinner we drove back to our apartment in Eric's jeep and went to bed early. The next morning, I could tell that Eric was so excited and tense about his upcoming skydive. He was more energized than I'd ever seen him before. Despite knowing that he could eat normally before a skydive, neither of us felt hungry. So, we headed straight to the drop location near Be'er Sheva at the northern edge of the Negev. Sometimes the take-off location and drop location were different but this time it would be at the same place.

We arrived punctually at 6AM at what appeared to be a small private airport featuring two runways, a pair of airplane hangars, and an office building. Nothing fancy. Ariel pulled up behind us two minutes later, parking adjacent to our vehicle outside the office. Three planes were parked on the runway: the smallest sported a single propeller on the nose, the next had one on each wing, and the largest bore two on each wing. I was a little surprised, although perhaps I shouldn't have been, when Julie exited Ariel's car. We exchanged morning greetings, and then Eric explained that he wanted us here this early to demonstrate how the parachutes were packed and to give us an overview of the equipment and plane. Ariel was positively glowing with anticipation, while Julie's face remained stoic. I immediately realized she was as skeptical about this endeavor as I was, but unlike me, she was not good at hiding her disapproval.

Once inside the office, Eric introduced us all to our pilot and flight instructor for the day. Both were former military buddies of his. The pilot, Boaz, and flight instructor, Joshua, were extremely experienced and ran a thriving business offering skydiving experiences to tourists. In fact, they had to squeeze us in. Despite their packed schedule, they'd made a special effort to accommodate us on short notice at Eric's request.

The instructional session lasted about two hours. By the end, Ariel had opted to dive "in tandem" with Joshua for his first jump, while Eric would dive solo. The larger four-engine plane was chosen for the day's jump. Joshua and Ariel would be hooked together just before their jump. Joshua mentioned that his "free fall" portion of the dive with Ariel would last about 40 seconds, but Eric could determine his own duration. At this point, I blurted out at Eric, "Just remember to pull the fucking cord!" All Eric did in response was flash a thumbs up and a broad smile. I realized he was clearly in his element.

At this point, Julie rushed up to Ariel, offering him a big kiss and hug. Despite Ariel appearing slightly embarrassed by it, I found it endearing—it clearly demonstrated her deep love and concern for him. Meanwhile, I fought an internal battle, suppressing an urge to rush to Eric, kneel down, grab him by the leg and plead with him not to go. But I knew that by doing so, while I might prevent him from going, I risked losing him completely. Regaining my composure, I snapped a photo with my cell phone of the flight group together before their departure. Seeing this, Julie also began taking photos and videos.

I must say, they all looked rather dashing in their jump uniforms and helmets. As a final point, the instructor asked Ariel and Eric if they needed to use the restroom, emphasizing that now was the time. He then turned to Julie and me, instructing us to return to the vicinity of the office. As the four "airmen" walked to the parked plane on the runway, both Julie and I were snapping photos and taking videos with our cellphones.

As the plane was starting to take off, I noticed a black Mercedes speeding towards the office. It was Jacob. He parked and came walking fast directly in our direction. This time he wasn't on his cellphone. I could tell by the look on his face he was worried and not happy. The first thing he said was if I realized if anything happened to Ariel all our deals were off.

I looked him straight in the eyes and said, "I don't think either Ariel or Eric gives a damn about that." His demeanor changed instantly. I could see that he immediately realized that he had over stepped and played it wrong. When I sensed this change in him, I added that for "the record" both Julie and I were against this but couldn't stop it. Julie chimed in, sharing how she made Eric promise to quit skydiving when they were dating. But she thought that since Eric and she were no longer together, she guessed that Eric thought the promise was no longer valid. Her statement hit me like a thunder bolt. I thought to myself that this whole thing was a test of our relationship. Eric knew I would be dead set against it. I then said in Eric's defense, "This was Ariel's wedding gift request. Eric was simply accommodating him." This seemed to stop Julie and Jacob in their tracks.

We all started to look at the plane high in the sky above us. It had initially headed north, almost out of sight, before veering back. Suddenly, we saw two dots drop from the plane.

We all took a breath. After what seemed an eternity—roughly a minute—one parachute opened, transforming the black dot into the silhouette of two men, almost floating down to earth on the parachute. Another minute of free-falling passed before, thankfully, the other parachute also opened, beginning its gentle descent. It was a perfect weather day for skydiving. As both parachutes, and their occupants, became clearer, I realized that Eric, having free-fallen longer, would land first, despite the other parachute carrying a heavier load.

Anticipating his landing spot, I found myself sprinting towards it. He guided himself to gently land with a thud about ten feet in front of me. He had a big grin on his face. I did not even give him a chance to undo his parachute harness as I threw myself into his arms, offering the tightest hug and deepest kiss I could muster which he returned with equal fervor. In an instant, we were covered by his white parachute. We stood there enveloped in billowing white silk, wrapped in each other's arms. I called him "my sexy he-man." I could tell as he pressed his body against mine that he was ready to make love right there and then, but I reminded him that we were not alone. As I took a step back, I simply said, "Keep that motor running." He looked mildly disappointed but understood.

Moments later, we heard the resounding sound of boots thumping onto the ground at the drop site nearby. We began disentangling ourselves from the white silk parachute while Eric unhitched his harness. Just in time, I emerged to see Ariel and Joshua standing where they had landed. Joshua was working on unhitching them from the parachute while Ariel waved at me, his face displaying a full-blown adrenaline-fueled grin, just like Eric's.

I didn't see Ariel for long because in the next instant, Julie threw herself onto him in a full embrace, obstructing my vision of him. Ariel, of course, immediately reciprocated. I knew they were both fine—Ariel more than fine! So, I turned back to Eric, who by now had unfastened himself and collected most of the parachute in his arms. He signaled me to follow him to one of the airplane hangars.

Once inside the hangar, he dumped the parachute equipment on a table and gestured for me to follow him to the rear. I noticed a room marked "toilet" where we were heading and started to smile, realizing what was coming. I knew it would have to be a quiet quickie. As soon as the door closed, we began making love. While making love I noticed a change in his body scent—he smelled like a wild, sexy animal. It was a huge turn-on for me.

Afterward, while walking back to our car and friends, I mentioned his sexy smell to him. He said he knew all about it. His explanation was that the exhilaration from skydiving releases so much adrenaline and excitement in the body that sweat glands produce a distinct smell, which many people find stimulating, likening it to the scent of an animal. "This energy has to go somewhere. And we both know where it just went!" he added.

Giggling like teenagers on a first date, we made our way back. However, I now dramatically changed my position on Eric going skydiving again. I decided he could go as often as he liked, just as long as I was there to meet him on the ground for the after party!

As we approached our friends gathered around our parked cars, I noticed that the atmosphere was much more relaxed and friendly. Jacob offered to take us all to lunch at Meatos in Tel Aviv, known to be the best steak place in the city. Since we all were famished by this time, we quickly agreed. Eric then asked Ariel about his first skydiving experience. Ariel responded enthusiastically, declaring it the most exciting thing he had ever done and the best day of his life. He thanked Eric profusely for the exhilarating wedding gift. When I asked Eric if I should tip Boaz and Joshua for their excellent service, he said he had already taken care of it.

As we drove off to lunch, I began to chuckle in the car. When Eric asked why, I was chuckling to myself. I answered that I think Julie was in for an adrenaline surprise tonight from Ariel. Eric just shook his head at the way my mind worked, but very soon started chuckling himself.

When we arrived at the restaurant, of course, Jacob was instantly recognized and a table was waiting for us. We quickly hit the men's and ladies' rooms to try and wash off the morning's dust and dirt and returned to our table looking considerably more fitting for such an elegant place. We ordered a huge lunch—more like a dinner really. I revealed to everyone that Eric and I had decided on Egypt for our honeymoon, but first needed to obtain our wedding license in the US. We settled on acquiring it and having the wedding conducted by a rabbi, all in New York City. Then, I mentioned to Ariel and Julie that we also wanted to attend their wedding here and their reception in NYC. However, we hoped to do this close together to avoid unnecessary traveling. Jacob cut in, assuring me this would be easier than I thought. He had plans to rent a large private plane for the round trip and everyone was invited on board. He then told Eric that this included his family as well. Not giving Eric an instant to think about it, I seized the opportunity and told Eric that this would be a great chance for me to get to know his family better. I smiled my most charming smile as I said this while I was actually thinking, "Hang me now!" Before Eric could read me, I quickly added that Eric and I wouldn't need the return trip because we were headed straight to Egypt from New York City. However, we both wanted to express our gratitude to Jacob in advance for his generous invitation to travel on the private plane.

Next, I asked Julie if she and Ariel had set their wedding date yet. She assured me that she was aware of our winter solstice deadline for the upcoming expedition to the Negev and would set the wedding date with Ariel very soon. As she spoke, I noticed her stunning round diamond ring. Before I could compliment her on the piece, she extended her hand across the table, revealing her engagement ring from Ariel! And yes, it was a replica of one of the twelve ten-carat pure white diamonds from the crown I placed on Ariel's head when we discovered King Herod's treasure. Impressed, Eric and I congratulated her in unison, exclaiming, "Mazel Tov!" That was what I said out loud. But actually, I thought to myself, "What an expensive ring!"

Jacob, as if sensing my inner thoughts about how expensive her ring must have been, swiftly shifted the topic. He shared that the transfer deed to our new house was on his desk and that he would sign it today. He continued that if Solomon confirmed that all the paperwork was completed, we could move into our new home tomorrow. Eric and I were thrilled.

In honor of this special occasion, I broke my usual practice of holding back from alcohol at lunch and ordered wine. I proposed a toast to our two daredevils—(and frisky—which I thought but did not say) —skydivers, grateful for their safe return. The group joined in, raising their glasses to my toast, and all echoed in unison the Hebrew toast, "L'Chaim—To Life!"

For the rest of lunch Ariel dominated the conversation by giving everyone a detailed description of how he had jumped out of plane and free fell for almost a minute before landing by parachute. He was overjoyed with his accomplishment. While this conversation was happening, Jacob sat silently listening with a smile. However, it was clear to me that he was realizing his son was now an adult and his control over Ariel's life was dwindling. Fortunately, Ariel had remembered to take pictures of all of us at this celebratory lunch.

After lunch we all departed for our respective homes or offices. Later in the day, Solomon called to confirm that the deed had been signed to our new home and we could move in tomorrow if we wanted. He requested that we stop by his office first to pick up the keys.

When Eric and I arrived home, we spent over an hour packing our "stuff" to leave the next day. I called the rental company from which we were leasing the apartment and paid off the remainder of the lease in full. The following day was a hectic one. Eric and I were both up early. He dropped me at Solomon's office to pick up the house keys and asked me to wait there as he had some errands to run. While I was waiting, I realized we were still a one-car couple. And that one was only a much beloved but nevertheless beat up old military jeep. So I asked Solomon for a Mercedes-Benz dealership recommendation. He informed me that if I knew which car model I wanted, the dealership could deliver it to our new house the next day. I provided him with the specifications—a black four-door coupe with brown leather interiors—and he promised to handle the paperwork and transfer the money.

Around noon, Eric returned to fetch me and the keys. We headed towards our new house with the back of his jeep laden with our "stuff". On the way there I mentioned that I had just purchased a new Mercedes, due to be delivered tomorrow. He was welcome to drive it anytime. Additionally, I suggested that it might be time for him to consider getting a new car as well, quickly adding that did not mean we should get rid of his current one. We had ample space at the new place to keep both vehicles. His reaction didn't register surprise. Rather, he seemed genuinely pleased. Being the intuitive man he is, he then asked, "Do you think we can afford a new Land Rover 90X?" His choice didn't take me by surprise—a Land Rover was quintessential Eric. I reassured him that he had more than enough funds in his account, reminding him that our last successful treasure hunt made him more than two million dollars. He should just ask Solomon to handle the purchase. For now, I suggested he draw the funds from my account and conserve his. Then, Eric pleasantly surprised me by proposing that he purchase my new car for me, and if I wished, I could buy his. He suggested this could be our joint engagement gifts to each other. I thought this was a brilliant idea. This conversation made me realize that we should create joint accounts as soon as we were legally married. When I voiced this idea, he looked puzzled. So, I clarified, what's mine is yours and what's yours is mine. Once married, I planned to set up a joint account for us. While he seemed a tad unsure about my proposition, I was confident he would thank me later.

As we pulled up to our new home, it was even more captivating than I remembered. The exterior of the house was a striking, modern architectural marvel, beautifully landscaped. Eagerly, we both hopped from the jeep and made a beeline for the entrance. Overcome with excitement, I fumbled with the keys to unlock the door. Once I managed to turn the key, the ten foot (32.8m) high double bronze doors effortlessly swung open to reveal what appeared to be acres of gleaming white marble. I was even more astounded than the first time (and only time) I had laid eyes on it. Eric was right behind me, quickly handing me a bouquet of flowers made of red anemones (poppies), white roses, and blue lilies. He then swept me off my feet and carried me across our threshold. I was more than surprised. I was stunned by his show of affection. When he gently lowered me against his muscled, athletic form, I found myself melting into his arms. As we shared a passionate kiss, I could sense our mutual love was overwhelmingly profound. I didn't even realize I was still clutching the bouquet of flowers. I don't remember how long we stood this way. Finally, we both had to catch our breath. The first thing I said was that I loved him, to which he responded that he loved me too. It was the first time we had expressed this sentiment to each other. After a while we let go of each other while still standing in the foyer of our beautiful new house. Then, almost simultaneously, we both said to each other, "Welcome Home!"

As my senses returned to me, the first question I posed to Eric was about the bouquet of flowers which seemed so out of character for him. He explained that he had briefly met his mother this morning at her place and she had insisted he give me a bouquet and carry me over the threshold of our new house. He then asked if I was aware that the red poppies in the bouquet were the national flowers of Israel. I answered that I had, but also, I confessed that the gesture had overwhelmed me and that I needed to reconsider my feelings about his mother, who had obviously accepted "us". When I told him this, I could tell he was pleased.

Turning to our surroundings, I suggested that we take a close look at what we just bought. Eric chuckled, "Too late now!" Eric first went to a utility closet in the back hall which I thought was a bit odd but emerged with the floor plans and schematic drawings of the house. Apparently, he had spoken to Solomon who had told him where they were kept. While he studied these, I walked around the first floor.

I immediately noticed that Jacob had left all the expensive custom furniture, along with the high-end crystal, china and cookware in the kitchen. He had only taken the artwork, just as we agreed. The most pleasant surprise of all was when I discovered that the bed linen was percale Egyptian cotton— the most expensive in the world.

Joining Eric in the kitchen, where he was still studying the house plans, I noted the perks of buying a house from a billionaire. His throwaways are most people's buys of a lifetime. Eric looked up at me when I said this with a smile on his face and said he had discovered something even better. While studying the plans he had discovered two rooms we had missed when Jacob had shown us the house. He explained that between the two first-floor master bedrooms was a safe room hidden behind what appeared to be a plain wall. He demonstrated by pushing a little lever in the upper corner of the wall, revealing a windowless room roughly the size of a small bedroom. He explained that we could hide in this room if we ever had intruders, and he was planning to turn it into our telecommunications center so we could also call for help.

Next, we walked out to our beautiful pool area which was surrounded by a high privacy wall. Eric pointed to something I had not noticed before: Attached to the house was a double wide sliding glass door leading to a fully equipped gym. We were both delighted at the prospect of our own private gym. However, Eric saved the best surprise for last. Back in the kitchen, he urged me to push against what I had assumed was a blank wall. To my astonishment, a door swung open, revealing a temperature-controlled wine room stocked with nearly a hundred bottles of wine. I suggested calling Jacob to double check about the wine, suspecting he may have forgotten to take it.

Finishing our tour, Eric emphasized the need for a robust security system beyond the existing front door lock. He proposed installing a state-of-the-art biometric and voice-based system that would eliminate the need for keys; I would only need to stand in front of an installed computer screen and speak a greeting to open the front door. I agreed, provided that the system wouldn't be prone to false alarms in lighting storms and wake us both. Eric assured me that such incidents were a thing of the past with these new systems. So I agreed and then told him the most important choice now was to pick a bedroom. We both picked the two adjacent downstairs master bedrooms and promised one another no matter where we hung our clothes or used separate bathrooms, we would always sleep together in the same bed! That in both our minds was not negotiable.

We spent the rest of the day unpacking and settling into our new home.

We found a supermarket on the outskirts of Haifa and stocked the kitchen, prepared a light dinner, and fell dead asleep in each other's arms. The following morning, I awoke to find Eric completing his new morning routine: an outdoor shower followed by laps in the pool. Not to be outdone, I also took a quick outdoor shower and cannonballed into the deep end of the pool. I continued by swimming several laps. I carefully timed my swim to finish with Eric's so we could make love on the steps in the shallow end of the pool—our first time in our new home. Neither of us bothered with bathing suits then or in the future due to the high stone wall covered with flowering vines surrounding the pool offering us complete privacy.

After that, I prepared a quick breakfast and Eric dashed out to catch up with Sam about our upcoming archeological expedition in the Negev. However, just as he was leaving, our two engagement presents—our new cars—arrived. Eric spent a few minutes signing paperwork, then drove off in his new Land Rover 90X, leaving me with my new luxury four-door Mercedes. I then contacted Solomon to confirm that all paperwork and insurance for the cars were in order.

I also called Jacob to thank him and discuss the wine he had left in the wine room. He told me to keep it but suggested he might borrow a few bottles for a party at some point. I asked him about maintenance services, and he promised to send over his contacts for me to interview and possibly hire. With that settled, he ended the call abruptly, his usual style.

Just when I thought I would have a few moments to myself to finish my second cup of coffee, my cell phone rang. It was Ariel, informing me that he and Julie had selected a date for their wedding in Israel and their reception in New York City. Actually, it was going to be a grand affair—three days of celebrations in Israel followed by a lavish reception in NYC.

What intrigued me most, though, was the location of the reception in NYC. Jacob had connections with a member of the Board of Directors at the American Museum of Natural History, and so, he was able to reserve the Rotunda. This colossal room is six stories high and nearly a NYC block wide, located just at the museum's main entrance overlooking Central Park. It housed gigantic skeletons of a Tyrannosaurus Rex in attack mode, locked in a battle to the death with a three horned Triceratops, along with a pair of Pterodactyls suspended high above them in hunting stance. I had been in awe of the place as a child and thought it would be an exciting and fun venue for a party. But this also meant that I needed to get everything in order for Eric and me. After congratulating Ariel once more, I quickly ended the call.

Next, I reached out to my niece in NYC for advice. She recommended a wedding/party planner she knew, and within the next five minutes, I was on the phone with Sheila, who I hired as our wedding planner. I explained to Sheila that we were all flying in on the same plane and required airport pick-ups. She recommended that we stay at the Pierre Hotel, which boasted beautiful views of Central Park, and I agreed. She proposed a schedule: dinner at a nice restaurant on the first night, a trip to City Hall for a legal marriage ceremony the next morning, followed by a

Reform Synagogue wedding ceremony. Neither Eric nor I were particularly concerned about the religious ceremony, but Eric felt it would please his mother. After the religious ceremony, we would need another dinner for everyone before attending the reception/dinner dance held the next day at the American Museum of Natural History. We could then choose to extend our stay in NYC or return on Jacob's private rental plane. I instructed Sheila to proceed with the arrangements, informing her that she was now our NYC point of contact. I provided her with Solomon's and Jacob's cell numbers. She also reminded me that we needed to purchase wedding rings for each other.

My head was spinning when she hung up. So I thought I would take a leisurely drive to Tel Aviv for a pleasant lunch by myself in the White City neighborhood where most of the art galleries were located. While there I again made a promise to myself to exclusively purchase artwork from Israeli artists for our new home. This was the first time I drove my new Mercedes. It was so much more comfortable than Eric's old jeep! I was also very pleased with myself that I was able to read and understand all the traffic signs in Hebrew. My study of Hebrew was paying off.

However, my memories from here on, of the upcoming two weddings, are somewhat hazy. Events unfolded rapidly, leaving a bit of a blur. I distinctly remember only the high points of the three day celebration for Ariel's and Julie's wedding which were the ceremony itself and the memorable reception. This grand event took place on the terrace of Jacob's home, close to ours. Ariel and Julie made a stunning couple standing there with the rabbi under the Huppah, a traditional Jewish white tent with the supporting poles intertwined with flowers, symbolizing the Tabernacle, which houses the presence of God. The ceremony culminated with Ariel stomping on the glass cup, traditionally covered in cloth, signifying the couple's hope that the couple will spend as many happy years together as it would take to gather and reconstruct the shattered glass. Despite Julie previously dating my Eric, I had decided to support this marriage wholeheartedly. After all, Ariel was not only strikingly handsome but more importantly had become a very good friend. And let's face it—he was also poised to inherit several hundred million dollars from Jacob. Julie could do worse! But you had to give her credit; she looked radiant beside Ariel and more than satisfied with her choice—a really beautiful couple. As a side note, I also recall Jacob's banquet staff emptied out almost all the wine he left us in our wine storage room for the wedding guests. But who cared about that?

At the post-wedding reception, aside from the significant wine consumption, I also remember that I met the Prime Minister of Israel again. I expressed gratitude for his support for our forthcoming archeological expedition to Mount Karkom. However, it was odd, I thought, that every time I speak to the Prime Minister both Eric and Sam made sure they are standing close behind me. Of course, I introduced them both to the Prime Minister. But they all said they already knew each other. I think that Sam and Eric thought that I might say something inappropriate which they would have to explain later. Would never happen! Anyway, as the PM walked away, he mentioned that I should remember to keep everything "by the book" in the Negev. I assured him I would.

As for our own wedding in New York City, it began with a relaxing flight from Tel Aviv on Jacob's rented private jet. I got to know Eric's mother, Miriam Jansen, and his brother and wife, David and Susan Jansen, much better. Coming from a military family, they were all directly or indirectly affiliated with the Israeli military. They were suitably impressed when I told them my late father had been the highest-ranking Jewish officer in the US Armed Forces, a full Colonel in the Air Force. I made a mental note that when we get back, I need to take Miriam for lunch—just the two of us—to get some more family stories about Eric.

Arriving in NYC three days before the reception at the museum, we had ample time to get married and do some sightseeing. I played tour guide for our group, showing them iconic landmarks such as the Statue of Liberty, the United Nations, and the Empire State Building's observatory deck. Yet, what I remember most was my surprise when Eric insisted on paying for our wedding rings at Cartier. Following this, we rushed to Brioni, a men's store specializing in custom fittings, and later that same day received our wedding outfits at our hotel suite. We secured our marriage license at the NYC license bureau and were wed under a Huppah by a rabbi in a quaint lower East Village synagogue recommended by my niece. I had never before seen Eric in a suit. He looked like he had stepped out of a fashion magazine. Our heartfelt wedding vows still echo in my memory as we looked into each other's eyes and said together, "You are mine, and I am yours. Forever!"

I also recall the time when Eric and I found ourselves with an afternoon to ourselves away from the group. I thought it would be a good idea to show Eric Central Park. It was a beautiful, crisp autumn day without a cloud in the sky. We strolled along pathways shaded by hundred-year-old trees until we reached the zoo. Eric particularly enjoyed watching the seals frolic in their open-air pool enclosure in the middle of the zoo especially when they splashed water onto unsuspecting tourists who had ventured too close. Not far from there were the lions and tigers in their outdoor cages, pacing incessantly. Numerous families were enjoying this spectacle. This family oriented atmosphere persisted as we left the zoo and passed the grand Bethesda Fountain, overlooking the beautiful boating lake with dozens of rowboats rowing on it.

However, as we crossed over a bridge leading to the lake's other side, the atmosphere shifted. The trails became narrower and more winding. The terrain grew hilly and the trees taller and denser. It felt as if we were now walking through an expertly choreographed old forest. The people in the park changed, too. Now there were almost no families, but only single men and some gay couples treading these secluded paths. Indeed, this was the famous gay section of the park called the Rambles. I was guiding Eric to the top of a massive glacial boulder right in the middle of it. The top of which was hidden from public view by thick forest undergrowth. From its peak we had a spectacular view of the entire skyline of buildings surrounding Central Park and the old stone Belvedere Tower at the Rambles' north end.

Looking at these stunning cityscape views, I mentioned to Eric that it was so private up here that many gay men sunbathed nude here in the summer—some even had sex up here. That suggestion was all it took for my young stud partner. I hadn't intended that we should make love here and now, especially since we have a luxury wedding suite waiting at the Pierre Hotel, but too late for second thoughts. It is always great to make love with Eric but this time I feared that any minute the police might arrest us for indecent exposure. It would have been so embarrassing! Luckily for us it was getting late and the park was emptying of people, so no one saw us. In fact, I noticed later when we descended that the area looked surprisingly deserted.

After this delightful interlude on the top of the rock, we realized we were going to be late for Ariel's and Julie's reception and dinner that night at the museum. So we made a mad dash back through the park to the Pierre, got ourselves ready, corralled our group and arrived at the Museum of Natural History on time. On the way to the museum, Eric and I ended up in separate limos, so I sat next to his mother, Miriam. En route, she told me she had never seen her son Eric happier. I was elated that she expressed this to me, and now fully understood that she supported my relationship with Eric and that she was a friend. I responded by inviting her to frequent dinners at our new place when we all get back.

The front entrance of the American Museum of Natural History, facing Central Park, spans one city block. The forty or so steps leading up to the exterior entrance, designed to resemble an ancient Roman temple, is nothing short of impressive. The impression you get as you ascend the steps is that something very special awaits inside, and it does not disappoint. What a stage for a party!

As we entered the Rotunda Hall, there was a receiving line which included Ariel, Julie, Jacob, and Julie's parents whom I had never met. Jacob had a humorous side. As I greeted him in line, he flicked an imaginary leaf and twig from my jacket's lapel with his finger and said, "There now. All clean." I started to laugh. Then I wondered, how did he know what happened in Central Park? But before I could ask, he leaned towards me and softly said, "Can't have any embarrassing moments in the Park. Can we?" I realized that this guy was so astute but a little scary too. His guests, along with family members, included the elite from the film and entertainment industry in Israel and the United States. This included a few well-known actors and actresses for sparkle but it was mostly the money crowd who financed and promoted films—the real power in the industry. I was sure that he was also using this wedding party as a business networking opportunity for himself and Ariel.

The Rotunda Hall of the museum had been formally set with large round tables and band at the far end with the dance floor in the middle surrounding the dinosaur exhibit. Each table was overflowing with a five-foot-high white rose centerpiece and gold china and crystalware. We were going to have dinner, drinks, and dancing! However, everyone's eyes were inevitably drawn to the terrifying dinosaur skeletons in the room. One could not miss the message of fang and claw that the skeletons of these beasts were sending. The fight to the death scene in the middle of the hall between a Tyrannosaurus Rex standing upright in attack position, the size of two buses with rows of six-inch (15.2cm) long blade-like teeth, locked in combat with a Triceratops the size of one bus with two, five-foot (1.5m) long needle pointed horns on its head and a third shorter but much stronger horn on the top of its beak, in defense position, set the tone of the Hall. Also, I cannot forget to mention the two flying skeletal Pterodactyls with twenty-five-foot (7.6m) wingspans in hunting mode, suspended three stories above us. I had adored the museum as a child, and unless they moved the rooms, I would still probably know the entire layout of the museum by heart.

Furthermore, I could always tell who were first time adult visitors. Their faces were always looking up, captivated by these skeletons especially the rows of six-inch (15.2cm) blade like teeth. Even later, when everyone was dancing, I saw their faces still fixated on these predatory beasts. Eric was among them. He had never been here before and was thoroughly smitten with the place.

He and I were seated at a table with our relatives. It was a great opportunity for me to further catch up with my nieces and nephew who had also attended our wedding. They also very much enjoyed talking archeology with Eric. Interestingly, I discovered that Eric enjoyed dancing, and he was quite good at it. There we both were, dancing slow dances and fast ones, always looking at each other but stealing a glance or two above us as we danced the night away under the gaze of the dinosaurs.

Eric and I departed the next day on a flight to Cairo from New York City. Jacob had a surprise meeting the next day, so the rest of the group had an extra day of touring NYC before returning on the private jet. Nobody complained, even if it meant extending the babysitters for their children one more day.

CHAPTER 6

AN OLD FRIEND AND AN OLD ENEMY

The nonstop flight from New York City to Cairo on EgyptAir lasted ten-and-a-half hours. My body had just started to adjust to the US East Coast time when we flew back to the Middle East. Fortunately, Cairo and Tel Aviv share the same time zone so there wouldn't be further local time zone adjustments after Cairo. Moreover, I planned on staying in this time zone for quite a while! We checked into the extremely chic Nile Ritz-Carlton Hotel, with luxury evident everywhere we looked. We had an incredible suite on a high floor with its own terrace overlooking the Nile River. The hotel was amazingly located in the center of the city and within a very short walk to the famous Egyptian Museum, the museum I was so fascinated to explore.

Despite my excitement about being in Cairo for the first time, I was physically drained from the travel and time change. Sensing my fatigue, Eric suggested I rest after I took a quick shower in our suite's spa-like bathroom. So I laid on our bed which was covered in exquisite percale Egyptian cotton linen and I was out cold in under five minutes. Several hours later, I woke up refreshed to find a short note from Eric on a small round table in our bedroom. It said to meet him at 5:30PM on the street corner to the left of the hotel's main entrance. I was to wear blue jeans, sneakers and a long sleeve shirt. Next to the note was some cheese and crackers, a bottle of ginger ale, and another of electrolyte infused water. Realizing it was almost time to meet, I hurried to get ready and head downstairs.

As I turned left leaving the hotel's entrance, I could not believe my eyes. In front of me at the street corner were two seated camels, one of which Eric was leaning against, grinning. With a smirk, I asked him, "Didn't you see the line of chauffeured cars waiting to take us wherever we want on the other side of the hotel entrance?" Eric's only response was, "You'll see. We'll need these where we're going. Plus, I know you've learned how to ride since you beat me in our camel race in the Negev!" As I mounted my camel, I admired the saddles. They were made of soft brown leather embossed with gold designs with one brass handle on top to hold, while layered beneath was padding which consisted of several brightly colored Persian rugs. I thought it made us look like pashas compared to the almost bareback camel race we had in the Negev.

As we began our journey through modern urban Cairo with Eric leading the way, he called out to me that his camel's name was Abdul and mine was Sarah. I immediately responded with feigned indignation, "Why do I get the girl camel?" Eric burst out laughing. I chuckled to myself that my partner has again proven he has such an odd goofy sense of humor. I then bent over my saddle so Sarah could hear me and assured her to never mind the guy leading us, she and I are going to become good buddies. So the next burning question on my mind that I asked Eric was, "Where the heck are we going on camels through a huge urban city like Cairo?" His reply was cryptic: "We are going to Egypt." Confused, I wondered, "Aren't we already in Egypt?" The sights and sounds of Cairo were all around us. As we moved through the city, crossing a bridge over the Nile River into what seemed like an older neighborhood with narrower streets. What I found surprising, though, as we lumbered through, was the people on the streets almost completely ignored us riding our camels. The good news was that because we were on camels we were able to navigate the nearly gridlocked traffic of modern Cairo. Nevertheless, it took almost an hour to reach our destination as the sun was setting.

We finally emerged from the crowded city, leaving behind the tightly knit houses, to behold the pyramids on the Giza Plateau. Immediately when our camels' feet touched sand, the whole feeling of the place changed. A serene quietness set in. I also noticed that there was a high metal fence between the raised plateau and modern Cairo but Eric guided us directly through a hole in it. As we approached the pyramids on the plateau, I noticed a stream of tourists and guides leaving the area from the side opposite our entrance. Even the vendors in front of the main tourist entrance were closing for the day. Eric mentioned that there was not going to be any sound and light show on the plateau tonight. By now, the sun had completely set, and it was darkness all around us except for the lights of modern Cairo twinkling behind us. The night can be so black before the stars come out.

I was growing slightly uneasy, realizing we were very soon to be quite alone in this strange yet magnificent place. I called to Eric, asking if everything was alright? He answered that we would arrive in just a few more minutes. Sure enough, less than five minutes later, we had arrived. But where, I did not know. We ordered our camels to sit and rest. Eric turned on his cell phone flashlight and suggested I do the same, gesturing for me to follow him. We carefully climbed ancient stone steps to the top of the remains of a ruined tower about fifteen feet (4.6m) high. While still completely dark outside, at the top of the tower, he tightly embraced me, his head and larger body further blocking my sight. Then he said, "Welcome to Egypt!"

With that, he stepped away and, as if on cue behind him, a full moon and a galaxy of stars behind it had risen. The vast Giza Plateau was now bathed in the brightest moonlight. The monumental pyramids of Giza—Kafre, Menkaure, and the largest, the Great Pyramid of Giza—as well as the Great Sphinx and the desert beyond, shimmered like polished silver in the reflected moonlight against the black velvet sky, studded with thousands of stars sparkling like pure white diamonds. These overwhelming monuments appeared almost new as the moonlight masked the age marks of more than five millennia. One of the Seven Wonders of the Ancient World lay before me. I had seen these pyramids and sphinx many times in photos and videos but they did not do justice to the reality. Now, they were so close and so monumentally immense, while we were so small and insignificant. The view was intoxicating, being so completely surrounded and overwhelmed by Pharaonic Egypt. It almost took my breadth away. It was an archeologist's dream.

And for a moment—just a moment—I imagined that I had been transported back to ancient Egypt. I don't remember how long I stared at this view, trying to take it all in, but I do remember Eric softly saying to me while looking at my stunned face, "It's time to come back." With that remark I was instantly back to reality. Then Eric added, "I know what my partner likes." Instead of thanking him for bringing me here, I asked him if he knew that he was the love of my life. He softly said, "Yes," he knew, and that I was his too. It was one of those intimate moments only people in love can share.

After that, my brain started to work again despite the awe and immensity of this place. So, I asked him what he thought we were standing on? He responded that his best guess was that it was a tower, once much higher, where the ancient priests used to study the stars—something like an astrological observatory. He then added that while we were on the subject of astronomy, I should look up at the three stars in the belt of the constellation Orion. I looked up and then down at the three nearby pyramids. I had studied the "Orion Correlation Theory" in college years ago but played dumb. I knew when I was about to be lectured and when to let my partner take the floor. Eric continued, explaining that many scholars believe the locations of the three major pyramids corresponded exactly to the three stars in the belt of Orion, especially if you rewind the heavens to 4,500 years ago.

I responded that he was so smart and there was no better place in the world to discuss this theory than right where we were standing. But I realized I was getting hungry and it was getting late. So, I suggested, "Why don't we discuss it over dinner?"

He agreed and asked me to lead the way down the ruined tower's cracked and battered ancient stone steps to our seated camels. As I turned to descend the stairs, I felt a strange sense of home, even though I had never previously been to Egypt. I thought we were going to ride the camels back to our hotel. However, just beyond the metal fence separating the Giza Plateau from the modern city of Cairo was a car and driver waiting to drive us back, along with two camel herders waiting to take Abdul and Sarah. Eric was giving everyone directions in fluent Arabic.

Once we were seated beside each other in the back of the car, I gave him a serious compliment on his exceptional Arabic skills. He humbly thanked me and added that he took pride in his ability to speak it with an Egyptian accent, a detail I wouldn't be able to pick up. His intellect truly amazed me at times. During our ride, our knees touched deliberately. Our eyes locked, and he softly suggested, "Let's wait until after dinner. I'm starving too."

We subsequently enjoyed an outstanding Middle Eastern dinner at our hotel's five-star restaurant called Bad El-Sharq, located on a lush terrace overlooking the Nile and the Egyptian Museum. Both of us savored a delicious roast lamb dish accompanied by an assortment of roasted vegetables and yogurt dip. The meal was reminiscent of the Israeli food I was familiar with, but what stood out were the two bottles of superb French wine. I was glad we were dining outside though. I am sure we both still smelled of camel and the desert from our recent adventure.

During dinner I couldn't help but gaze at the façade of the Egyptian Museum across the square. It looked just the same as it did in the old film called "The Mummy" with the actor Boris Karloff. I was enthralled and begged Eric that we needed to visit the museum first thing tomorrow. He agreed but with a warning it might take the entire day to explore, given the plethora of other sights. Nevertheless, I did not care. It was the mecca for any Egyptologist boasting the most extensive collection of ancient Egyptian artifacts in the world. And it was just across the street! We retired to our suite after dinner, showered, made love, and fell asleep in each other's arms.

The next morning, we awoke early, fully rested, and ready to embark on our next Egyptian adventure. Eric, as always, had meticulously planned and organized our day.

After breakfast at our hotel, we strolled across El Tahrir Plaza to the grand entrance of the Egyptian Museum. As we passed through the massive bronze doors, I caught my breath. Staring at us was the most impressive collection of ancient Egyptian artifacts on earth. The massive museum exhibit rooms designed like Egyptian temples from ages past. So all the objects were shown "in context" so to speak. To say the least, the presentation was nothing short of dramatic. We spent most of the day examining and discussing the exhibits. Eric had an encyclopedic knowledge of what we were seeing as he guided me through the museum.

Eric saved the gold treasure room of the Pharaoh Tutankhamun for the final room of the day. As soon as I entered the room, the strong smell of fragrant incense filled my nostrils, hitting me like a brick. I turned to Eric and told him this was the smell of the court in the palace of King Tut. Eric, puzzled, asked how I knew that. I elaborated, noting that the incense almost mirrored the correct blend of myrrh, frankincense, and cinnamon but in my opinion, not quite. Moreover, the most important ingredient the museum curators missed was the fruit of a particular palm tree that grew in the farthest reaches of the Upper Nile. When it was mixed with the incense and burned in the correct proportion it would create a beautiful pink haze in the room. However, if they mixed and burnt the same fruit later in the growing season the result would be a lovely purple colored haze. Eric was stunned at my assertive comments. He again asked me how I knew this. I answered that perhaps I remembered it from reading a research paper. He turned and looked straight at me. He told me that was impossible. He continued that this release of incense was a very recent museum initiative to enhance its visitors' experience. And that the incense itself was based on years of analyzing various seeds and powders found in canopic jars from ancient tombs. And the technique of actually recreating this ancient incense was based on very recent, and modern DNA research. And no research paper that he knew had published these findings yet. I just shrugged my shoulders as if to suggest then, I had no idea how I knew.

Nonetheless, I did remember to thank him for updating me about the museum's incense initiative. I added that I had also just confirmed my hunch about King Tut and the Exodus story. Eric knew that my last hunch had led to the discovery of King Herod's treasure so he became very quiet and listened intently to what I was about to say. I motioned him to take a good look around the room, filled with golden treasures from Tut's tomb. Eric noted that the tomb appeared loaded with golden artifacts. I then motioned him to look at a glass case housing a large gold box, the exterior adorned with intricate designs seemingly carved into solid gold. It was clear that Eric was missing what was apparent to me.

Quietly, I pointed out that all these golden artifacts in the room, with the exception of King Tut's solid gold mask and a few small figurines were not solid gold. They were only wooden objects sheathed in gold foil, exquisitely designed and hammered onto the wood.

Then I asked him, "What conclusion should we draw from this?" Eric said nothing. So I continued, "Let's assume that Egyptian wealth at the time was mostly based on vast quantities of gold looted from Egyptian raids on Nubia in the South." When I said raids, I meant huge boatloads of gold sailing the Nile, returning to Egypt. I continued that this room in front of us, filled with gold objects, seems like a significant amount of gold to us. Archeologists have actually determined that King Tut was buried with 264 lbs. (120 kg) of gold. Yet, if my hunch was correct, there was hardly any gold in this tomb compared to the wealth that was Egypt. "Why?" I asked, as Eric still stared blankly at me. So I answered my own question, "The gold in this room was what was left behind after the Hebrews 'plundered Egypt' of its gold and silver. And King Tut died too soon before the gold could be replaced. Moses, a former Prince of Egypt or at least a senior advisor at court, knew exactly where the gold was stored. So when the Pharaoh Tutankhamun told him to take the gold and silver of Egypt and leave, he did—almost all of it!" I now had a very strong hunch that King Tut was the Pharaoh mentioned in the Bible and I intended to prove it.

Eric was nonplussed at this hunch of mine. All he could say was that there were so many gaps in my theory or hunch which would be impossible to prove.

I responded that our upcoming archeological expedition to Mount Karkom might very well prove my hunch about it being the biblical Mount Sinai, but also what happened to 'the plunder of Egypt' by the Hebrews mentioned in the Bible. In the meantime, I had developed a very strong urge to visit the Valley of the Kings. So I asked him if we could go there the following day and visit the tomb of King Tut as well as the tombs of the two pharaoh's who in turn succeeded him: Ay, Tut's Grand Vizier and Horemheb, Tut's Commander in Chief of Tut's army and chariot corps. Eric agreed and said that the quickest way to get to the Valley of the Kings was to fly to Luxor, the modern name for ancient Thebes and return to Cairo the same day by plane.

When Eric agreed, he also warned me that it would be a grueling travel day to accomplish it all. I didn't care. Once I get focused on one of my hunches, time, cost, or my own health take a back seat to my new quest.

The next thing I remember about our trip to Egypt was descending the well-lit steps by myself and facing the open stone sarcophagus where the mummy of the pharaoh lay in the depths of King Tut's tomb. Eric was discussing or arguing about something outside with our local tour guide that we had to hire to be permitted to visit the Valley of the Kings. Since it also seemed not to be a busy tourist day, I found myself alone with the King in his tomb for a few minutes. As I stood by his sarcophagus looking down at the dried-up mummy of this crippled boy king, the strangest thing happened. I could swear I smelled the ancient incense of his royal court again. My conscious brain knew that this could not be happening. Yet I realized that somehow, I knew him and not just from photos and videos of the famous discovery of him and his tomb. But I actually realized that I knew all about him. Among my many thoughts were that I knew he died in the year 1325 BCE which meant he died over 3,300 years ago. But it felt to me like it happened just yesterday. A minute or so later, Eric appeared by my side as I was staring at the mummy. He asked me, "So what do you think of the most famous mummy in the world?"

I thought for a moment and then responded, "I believe the Pharaoh Tutankhamun had a momentous secret which no one has guessed until now." I then asked if he also smelled the ancient incense and saw the pink haze surrounding the mummy. Moreover, I spontaneously added, "There was always a pink glow in the presence of the Pharaoh." He shook his head to indicate no and looked at me as if something was wrong with me. Eric then placed his hands on my shoulders, looking at me straight in the eyes, he shook me to bring me back to reality while saying that I was the most metaphysically hypersensitive person he had ever met. I was a bit shocked at his observation because I hadn't realized this about myself. However, I responded by framing my gut feelings or whatever they were as a hunch to him. Thus, I continued to explain that the Pharaoh Tutankhamun whose mummy lay before us, was worshipped as a living God on earth by the mightiest nation in the world at the time. Not only was he the Pharaoh of the Exodus, but I also believe he actively helped his friend Moses and the Hebrews leave Egypt unharmed. Yes, it was evident looking at his mummy that he was physically crippled, but I believed his mind was sharp as a tack. And more astoundingly, he was actually a secret monotheist who worshipped the One God, the same belief that the Hebrews held.

I continued that when he assumed the throne as a boy of nine, he was forced to denounce his beloved father, the Pharaoh Akhenaton, as a heretic, as well as his own belief in the One God. Consequently, he banished the priests of the one true God and reinstated the pagan priests of Amun, leading to the exile of Moses in Sinai. As he aged, he likely realized he would never father a child to succeed him. This, I believed, was evidenced by the several stillborn children found in this tomb with him. He also knew that after his death, there would be a bloody succession struggle for the throne. To ensure the belief in the One God survived, he gave the Hebrews enough time to escape by engineering that Ay, his Grand Vizier, who was a doddering old fool by all accounts, would succeed him first. He knew Ay would not rule long and indeed he did not. This was to delay the succession of Horemheb, the Commander of Tut's army, including Egypt's renowned chariot corps, who Tut knew was quite capable of exterminating the Hebrews for their belief in the One True God. To further weaken Horemheb, the Pharaoh Tutankhamun gifted the Hebrews Egypt's gold reserves. I believe his reasoning was that if Horemheb lacked gold, he could not pay his soldiers! This also diverted Horemheb by forcing him to conduct more raids on Nubia to bring back more gold, thus creating further delays to enable the Hebrews to leave Egypt in peace and establish themselves in Canaan. Additionally, I think Moses knew of the plan and possibly helped the young Pharaoh Tutankhamun conceive it. After all, the Bible tells us that Moses was raised in the court of "Pharaoh". I believe it was the court of Tut's father, Akhenaton, the world's first ruler who believed in the One God and who tried and failed to turn Egypt away from paganism. Hence, Moses knew both men well.

As I looked at Eric's face, I could tell he thought his partner had gone crazy. So I softened my statements by emphasizing that, of course, what I just said was a hunch which I plan to prove. We then climbed the stairs and exited the tomb of "King Tut".

Next, Eric showed me the tomb of the Pharaoh Ay in the Valley of the Kings. This was a small tomb which had been ransacked and desecrated ages ago. Nothing of any importance remained. As we departed, I thought to myself how the state of this tomb was so appropriate for Ay as a ruler and as a man. But I said nothing to Eric about my thoughts on the matter.

Finally, we arrived at the tomb of the Pharaoh Horemheb. It consisted of several rooms with hieroglyphics painted on the walls. Instead of being chiseled in relief, the images were simply painted, which Eric found odd for a pharaoh's tomb, attributing it to the haste with which the tomb was prepared due to the pharaoh's short reign. The tomb had also been looted and the body destroyed according to Eric. I immediately thought that it was quite possible that the people who looted this tomb and destroyed his body very likely knew its occupant. He was never well liked. But again, I said nothing to Eric about my opinion on this. The good news was that the painted hieroglyphs were in very good shape and easy to read. So I asked Eric to translate some of what was written on the walls about the pharaoh, but especially to show me the cartouche of the Pharaoh Horemheb.

I immediately focused on Horemheb's cartouche which was his name written in hieroglyphics. However, his cartouche seemed oddly incorrect to me. It was all over the walls of the tomb. There were actually four rooms that seemed rather large when you were looking for something about an inch (2.5cm) by two inches (5.1cm) in size painted on them. I knew Eric thought I had truly lost my mind when I started scouring the walls of the tomb, looking at every cartouche of the Pharaoh Horemheb that I could find. Finally, I turned to Eric and said that if he wanted, he could wait outside for me since the hunt for what I was looking for could take a while. Notwithstanding the fact that I did not know what I was looking for!

Once more, I was in a tomb all alone, and because it was not a particularly busy tourist day, and due to the fact that this tomb was considered a minor tomb for a minor pharaoh, there were not a great number of tourists interested in seeing it. Meanwhile, Eric stood outside speaking to our guide. He was probably telling the guide that his partner had gone insane but was harmless and would emerge from Horemheb's tomb when he was ready.

I examined every cartouche of the pharaoh that I could find. There were hundreds of them. Finally, near the corner of the back room of the tomb, I saw a pile of sand on the floor that hid the bottom two feet of the tomb's wall. I cleared away the sand and at last, I knew I had found what I was searching for: The cartouche of the Pharaoh Horemheb with a snake carved at the top of it. His other cartouches had no snake image in them.

I thought to myself, "There you are. I knew I would find you." He had been such a snake in life, ready and willing to exterminate anyone who believed in the One God. I also knew in my gut that it was very likely that he either directly or indirectly assassinated the Pharaoh Tutankhamun and usurped the throne. So, without hesitating, I began urinating against the side of tomb, directly hitting the cartouche with the snake dead center. As I did this, I said aloud, "This is a message from the Pharaoh who you murdered and who wanted me to give it to you. And wherever you are, I hope you receive it loud and clear!" As I walked out of the tomb, my conscious self had no idea why I had just done that—but somehow, I knew I had to do it.

When I met Eric and our guide on the path at the front of the tomb, I told them I am ready to go and asked them what was next? Eric asked me if I had found what I was looking for. All I said to him was I am more convinced than ever that my hunch was correct about King Tut and the Exodus story. After that he asked me if I wanted to see some of the much larger, more impressive tombs in the Valley of the Kings. But I said, "No. I have seen what I came here to see."

Next, we decided to visit the Temple of Karnak, the power center of the priests of Amun. The temple complex was immense. It was built to impress and it still does. Eric explained that the temple complex, located on the East side of the Nile in Luxor (ancient Thebes), was built over a period of two thousand years and covered an area of 200 acres(81 hectares) including several different temples, halls, and courtyards. It included the Great Hypostyle Hall which was a vast hall supported by 134 massive columns, each over 70 feet (21.4m) tall. I spent the rest of the day looking up at monumental architecture and obelisks that almost took my breath away. I told Eric that I had to give the ancient Egyptians credit. They certainly knew how to "work rock!"

We took the last return flight of the day to Cairo and arrived at our hotel tired and famished. We were too tired to go anywhere else in town, so we had another great meal at our hotel. As we lay down in bed to sleep, Eric turned to me and softly said that he needed to leave me alone tomorrow. But he promised he would try to be back for dinner, but definitely intended to sleep here with me tomorrow night. In the meantime, he asked me not to worry and enjoy tomorrow. And please not to call him. He said this to me as I was falling asleep.

I was so extremely tired from our full day of sightseeing that I thought what he said to me was a dream until I woke up the next morning to find Eric's side of the bed empty. I sat up from the bed instantly as I tried to get my bearings and remember exactly what he had said. When it hit me, I was worried about him and furious at him at the same time. Every fiber in me wanted to call him on my cellphone, but I didn't since he had asked me not to call. My thoughts were focused on the possibility that this might be a Mossad assignment. The more I thought about it the more I was convinced that it was. Eric was after all, a major in the Mossad. And I would not put it past them to use our honeymoon as a cover for some mission.

I spent the rest of the day trying to pass the time. I walked over to the Egyptian Museum again. But this time I looked at the exhibits but did not really see anything. I spent less than an hour inside the museum. I wasn't hungry but had a light lunch at the hotel just to pass the time. I had a massage at the hotel spa but it failed to relax me. Finally, I returned to our room to try to enjoy the view of the Nile River from our terrace and wait for Eric. On our terrace, I reached a decision on what we were going to do next. We were going to leave here as soon as possible.

Sure enough, around dinner time, the door of our room opened and there stood Eric. The instant I saw him, I knew he was very stressed and fatigued. In fact, I had never seen him like this before. Of the many scenes (most of them not very nice) between us that I had imagined would take place when he returned, all we did was take one look at each other and quickly deeply embraced each other. We said nothing for a long time but stood embracing each other while standing in the middle of the room. I realized as we embraced, he was still mine and I was still his. I also realized that it was critical for both of us to destress like this. It was as if he was returning home from an alternate reality that I wasn't allowed to see.

Finally, I suggested that maybe he should take a shower and put on some new clothes. It would make him feel better. He agreed and, afterward, came out on the terrace to join me looking at the magnificent view of the Nile River and Cairo at night. My younger blond hunk of a husband looked like an action movie star on that romantic terrace.

He spoke first when he asked if I remembered that he had another job and sometimes that job required him to be away and he wouldn't be able to explain why or where. I replied, "I remember." He continued that this was one of those times.

I knew what I said next was critical to our relationship. So I softly said that I was getting a little bored with Egypt and thought it might be a good idea if we flew back to Israel tomorrow. I was really thinking that I had to get him out of the country as soon as possible before the police knocked on our hotel room door. He smiled that great smile of his and said that was exactly what he was going to recommend we do. But he added, would I mind if we could catch the last flight from Cairo tonight to Istanbul, change planes, and have breakfast tomorrow at our new home in Israel? All I said was that I could be packed in fifteen minutes. After all, I was eager to organize our archeological expedition as quickly as possible upon returning. Moreover, the Prime Minister gave Eric and Sam that assignment, which diminished the possibility of any dangerous side Mossad assignments. Eric surprised me as we were leaving our hotel room when he revealed that he had already booked our flights. All I said to him was, "I like it when great minds think alike!"

But it also occurred to me to question who manipulated whom about our early departure. I knew Eric had proven his ability more than once to know what I thought even before I had completed the sentence. Anyway, our return flights were uneventful. It would be good to get home again. Eric and I fell fast asleep as soon as our flight took off from Cairo to Istanbul and again on the flight from there to Tel Aviv.

CHAPTER 7

MOUNT KARKOM—HERE WE COME!

Both of us arrived back in Tel Aviv feeling rested. Sam met us at the airport and drove us home. As he chauffeured, he mentioned that he had almost completed the arrangements for our archeological expedition to Mount Karkom; only one more government agency's approval was required. He asked Eric to accompany him the following day to settle this. Additionally, he suggested that we have a team meeting at our lawyer's office in Jerusalem the day after. Naturally, I agreed and decided to contact Solomon and Ariel to arrange the meeting that very day. Sam also relayed how much he and his wife Alisa had enjoyed their time in New York City and thanked Jacob and Ariel personally for the invitation. But I was no fool. I knew his real intention was to debrief Eric on Eric's Mossad assignment in Cairo. But I held my tongue. He dropped us off, saying he would see us soon.

Upon entering our architecturally stunning new house, we didn't even unpack. Eric headed straight to the pool at the back, shedding his clothes as he went. I followed suit. After a quick poolside shower, we both plunged naked into our pool, enclosed by a high privacy wall adorned with flowers and trailing vines. After swimming a lap, Eric joined me, and we made love. When we finished, I told him that making love to him always felt like our first time. Chuckling, he replied that he felt the same way about me and guessed the honeymoon phase was still going strong. I responded saying that it would never be over for me. He smiled at this and swam away to finish his laps. Meanwhile, I exited the pool with a plan to unpack, stock up on groceries, and surprise Eric with my home cooked paprika chicken and side dishes—our first home cooked meal in the new house. There's a saying that the way to a man's heart is through his stomach and I knew that route well. I pride myself on being a damn good cook when I want to be.

Moreover, today would be my first experience grocery shopping in an Israeli supermarket. I considered it a daring move not to bring my interpreter—Eric—along, but I believed I could manage. Shopping at the Tiv Ta'am supermarket near our house turned out to be a breeze, and the staff was extremely helpful. I chose this supermarket because Eric had informed me that this chain was the largest purveyor of non-Kosher meats and items in the country. Feeling like I was home, I drove my new Mercedes, granting us both some much-needed alone time, which is beneficial in all relationships—safe alone time, that is, without anyone attempting to kill one of us!

Dinner turned out fantastic. Eric ate it voraciously. He loved my home cooking, and the aroma of roasted paprika chicken filled our house, making it feel like a real home. This in my mind dotted the eye in our relationship!

As Sam requested, I summoned our team to meet at Solomon's law office in Jerusalem the day after Eric and Sam would meet. The purpose of this gathering was to review and update the progress of organizing our forthcoming archeological expedition to Mount Karkom in the Negev. With the winter solstice approaching rapidly, I wanted everything in place. Early the next morning Eric drove his new Range Rover to meet Sam, having spent most of the previous night familiarizing himself with his new car's instruction manuals. Before his departure, we agreed to dine in Haifa that night to explore the restaurant and bar scene. I used my time that day to interview and hire a landscaping company recommended by Jacob and a housekeeping couple introduced by a personnel agency Jacob knew. Eric returned from his meetings, stating everything went smoothly and he would discuss it in detail at tomorrow's meeting. We then enjoyed a pleasant dinner at a small restaurant in Haifa that Eric knew, drove home, made love, and fell asleep in each other's arms. I chuckled to myself, thinking that making love to my handsome younger partner was always such "hard" work, but somebody had to do it!

Eric insisted on driving us to our team's meeting the next morning in his new Range Rover rather than have me drive mine. I spent my time driving to Jerusalem listening to Eric as he explained the technical manuals of his new car. I was glad he passionately enjoyed his new toy. Of course, I listened attentively as a good partner should, but was relieved when we arrived. I have zero interest in auto mechanics.

Fortuitously, the team was all assembled and ready to begin when we entered Solomon Levine's conference room. I could tell by their expressions that there was news to discuss. In addition to Eric, our expert archeologist and myself; Solomon, our lawyer, was present, as well as Ariel Kurtz, our official photographer, video and film expert; Sam Reichman, president of one of Israel's largest GPR companies and our most technically savvy expert on locating buried relics; and Jacob Kurtz, who was also present via a Zoom computer connection. He was the one bankrolling our expedition and was also a master in advertising and promotions. To my surprise, Ariel had also invited Julie, his new wife, to attend. Ariel noted my surprise and asked if we all didn't mind Julie being there. He explained that before she became his wife, Julie was his technical assistant, and since this expedition would be more complex than our previous one, he thought it would benefit his productivity if she could hear our strategy first hand. All team members, including myself, agreed that we had no objection to her attending team meetings.

Sam opened the meeting, wanting to update us all on the approval process, the expedition supplies, and transportation issues. He explained that permission for our archeological expedition to search for relics on or around Mount Karkom, potentially proving the mountain was indeed the biblical Mount Sinai, had been approved despite its sensitive location near the Egyptian/Israeli border and religious implications. Fortunately all the necessary Israeli ministers had signed off on it. These included the Director of Israel's Antiquity Authority and National Treasure Department; the Director of Israel's Civil Authority which controls the national parks; and the Director of the Israel Museum. He mentioned, however, that the permission granted did not include exploring the interior of the mountain's cave where the burning bush was supposedly seen. Also, the Ministry of Defense had permitted our use of their nearby military training area, as it won't be in use during our stay in December. Lastly, they had agreed to lend us two Chinook military helicopters to transport our team and supplies back and forth from their Negev training site. Sam added that military vehicles at the training site would be available for us to move our equipment to our actual campsite.

However, he continued to explain that this military involvement came at a cost. The expedition would have to cover the fuel costs for both the helicopters and military vehicles which could be substantial due to the helicopters' high fuel consumption. At this point, Jacob interjected to say these were legitimate expenses and he would pay them. We all applauded upon hearing this. Sam further revealed that two military airmen, who were also amateur archeologists had volunteered to assist us during our stay in the desert. Their names were Jethro and Gershon. We also discussed the costs of renting tents, storing food in the desert, maintaining hygiene, and sanitation equipment. The helicopters would be tasked with hauling in water, as well as removing waste and port-a-potties. Sam emphasized that after we depart, there should be no trace of our campsite. However, we were permitted to excavate but not on the top of Mount Karkom. Also, Ariel and Sam both approved of the large helicopters, given the ample space they offered to transport their equipment to the remote dig site.

Finally, towards the end of the meeting, Sam mentioned that there was one more item we needed to cover. I noticed that even though he discussed the item at open table with everyone present, I sensed that both he and Eric were focused directly on me. Sam mentioned, as matter of factly as he could that there would be an orthodox rabbi joining us on site. The Prime Minister had recommended his presence to avoid any potential desecration of artifacts we might uncover. Eric then clarified that we had already met the rabbi's younger brother, Moshe Ben-Levy, who served as our guide during our Temple Mount tour. I recalled Moshe as being very gracious and knowledgeable. Eric added that the rabbi's name was Asher Ben-Levy, who, in addition to being an ordained rabbi, also held a degree in archeology. Moreover, Asher was reputed to be a good cook and was eager to serve as the expedition's cook. I responded, saying he sounds perfect. I had yet to understand exactly why he was joining us and to whom he actually reported. However, I did ask the question about the Prime Minister 's use of the term "desecration". Jacob explained that while our discovery of King Herod's crown jewels during the last expedition was financially rewarding, many people were upset by the team's filmed 'fashion show' wearing the jewels. They perceived it as highly disrespectful, if not outright desecration. He quickly added, "Please, let me be clear, I was not one of them."

Lastly, Sam said that Asher would meet us on the plane when we all fly to the dig site. I told the team all that remained was for us to pick a date. Sam suggested we depart at the end of next week to allow ample time for setup and exploration before the winter solstice. As the room filled with excitement, I exclaimed, "Mount Karkom, get ready! Here we come!" With that, the meeting was adjourned.

Ten days later we all took off from Hatzor Air Base, situated in central Israel. It was exhilarating for me to be in one of these immense Chinook helicopters. In the air I could survey the entire expanse of Israel from one end to the other. I could tell everyone else on the team was equally captivated by the view, as they all had their eyes fixed on the windows. Even Sam and Eric were engrossed in the sky-high vistas, despite having made two previous trips to set up our campsite before our arrival. The previous ten days had been extraordinarily busy, dealing with the logistics for the expedition. Although I had offered to help, my offer was very politely declined. I gathered that my expertise wasn't required and that I might "just get in the way". On this flight, I also met our newest team member for the first time, the orthodox Rabbi Asher Ben-Levy. He struck me as a very affable fellow. And my initial impression was positive as, before we landed, he had volunteered to prepare all our meals—a task I was more than happy to pass on! The only stipulation was that all meals had to be kosher, which presented no issue for me. However, despite his attempts to charm and ingratiate himself with the team, I could sense that he was a force to be reckoned with.

CHAPTER 8

HOLY WATER?

Eric and I bolted upright from our cots in our desert tent, exchanging incredulous looks as if to ask, "What on earth just happened?" Having slept fully clothed the previous night, we just had to hastily put on our boots before rushing out of our tent to see what Ariel was shouting about. At first, we stared in disbelief at the dried-up old riverbed that now flowed with water through the valley in front of the mountain, still considered sacred by many. This was no raging torrent of water, mud and debris so common in desert flash floods but crystal clear water gently rolling along beckoning us to swim or drink, revealing ancient riverbanks as it passed. The team members could hardly believe their eyes. By the side of the freshly flowing river, Sam did a quick water toxicity test to confirm that the water was safe. It was. Finally, Eric voiced the question we were all thinking, "What happened and how did this water get here?" At the same time, I thought to myself but didn't voice out loud, "The real question is: What does it mean? Is it a sign from God?"

Before anyone could utter another word, I impulsively turned, ran back to the tent, grabbed my bar of soap, a towel, and my canteen. I then ran to the edge of the river and quickly waded in, fully clothed, considering there was a lady present. Moreover, I didn't want to waste time undressing given the uncertainty of how long the water would flow. The cool water swirling around me felt incredibly refreshing and was surprisingly clear. Now I turned to face my somewhat dumbstruck companions and yelled, "Come on in, the water's fine! I don't know about you all, but I desperately need a bath. I have to wash the desert sweat and cobra blood off me and my clothes!" At this, my comrades' frozen stares melted as they all simultaneously turned, ran back to their tents, collected their things, and jumped in. I could hear their splashes behind me as they leaped into the gently flowing river. I had already turned away to swim closer to the center of the river, now chest deep, and felt cleansed by it—both physically and spiritually. I remember submerging my entire body and reemerging from the water to behold one of the most strikingly beautiful rainbows in the sky I had ever seen.

Unusually, this time, I could see where one end of it ended (or began). It was dead center on the rock face from last night that I had found and on which I had asked Sam to attach his homing device. I immediately turned to my fellow team members and exclaimed, "Look, everyone, a beautiful rainbow pointing to the place we need to explore today!" Then I added, "Isn't this a sign from God? He's showing us the way!" Standing in the flowing water in the middle of a bone dry desert, I realized that this water too was a sign from God. Everyone smiled and nodded in agreement, except Asher. He looked as though I'd hit him with a hammer—very unsteady. He quickly turned, climbed out of the water, grabbed his towel, and retreated to his tent—presumably to start making breakfast. I also thought it was time to get out of the river, especially since I noticed that the water had started to recede. As I was climbing out of the river, I paused for a moment to fill my canteen with this miraculous water. As I did this, I found myself wondering whether the water from this river would be considered holy water in ancient times?

Indeed, we all had many questions about the water's origin. As we dried off from our morning swim, discussions and theories started to flow. It became the main topic of conversation over breakfast. Our general consensus was that there hadn't been an actual river here for thousands of years, and its reemergence must have been due to a freak, heavy rainstorm somewhere in the desert. But for me, I was convinced that God had sent us a strong sign, pointing the way to a significant discovery. Fortunately, Ariel and Julie had filmed the bizarre river in the heart of the Negev, capturing enough landmarks in the footage to erase any doubt about where the event had occurred. I was grateful they did, for by the end of breakfast the river had dwindled to a trickle, and by the next day, I was certain it would be a dried-up old riverbed once more.

Eric and Sam were both very confident that a downpour somewhere in the nearby mountains had caused this sudden flood. So, I decided to meet science with science. I simply suggested that what happened this morning helped to prove my suspicion that Mount Karkom was indeed the Sinai of the Bible. I explained that the petroglyphs atop the mountain depict a variety of large prey animals and predators. This meant the area around here more than 3,000 years ago had to be consistently well-watered to support such wildlife. It also indicates that after journeying across the Sinai desert, Moses needed water from this river for his herds and livestock, as well as the Hebrew people themselves. I believed that Moses and his acolytes, who were younger Egyptian priests of the One God, were very familiar with the Sinai desert and timed their arrival here about a month before the winter solstice. My hunch was that Moses considered the burning bush phenomenon as the perfect backdrop to introduce the Ten

Commandments to the Hebrews for the first time; the awe-inspiring nature of which making the laws more memorable. I knew this secular explanation would appeal to Sam, Eric, Ariel, and Julie. I also knew that Asher, my orthodox rabbi friend, might consider my hypothesis borderline blasphemous and definitely unprovable.

Reflecting later, I thought the day had started very early and on a rather intriguing note. And for the first time in many days, I also felt clean and, thus, reenergized. As breakfast ended, I asked everyone to reconvene at the tent in half an hour to plan our strategies for our new dig site that day. I stressed the urgency of our mission. If we didn't discover something soon, our time here would end, and we'd return home with only some interesting desert camping stories to tell. When we returned to our tent after breakfast, my first step was to call Jacob and update him on what had transpired. I confessed that my initial choice for the dig site was incorrect, but I now had a strong hunch about a new location. I then informed him that despite our initial failure, we had decided to extend the expedition by two more days to verify the new site. He understood but wanted to know how Ariel and Julie were doing. I answered him in a single word, "Indispensable!" I knew he would appreciate that and it was also true. We then ended the call.

Since we already knew the site where we wanted to explore, Sam led the morning meeting on how to discover what lay inside our new, relatively small mountain target. First, he recommended we employ an aerial drone to survey it. We could then decide our next steps. Fortunately, he had brought a drone on which he could attach a ground penetrating radar unit. Concurrently, it would also capture aerial photos of the surface of the mountain. He assured us that he could have everything ready to launch in under two hours and the process would take another two hours to complete. He was going to need both Jethro and Gershon, our young helicopter crew members, to assist in the setup. Additionally, he informed us that the images captured by the drone would be immediately visible on his computer. We were further fortunate that both Jethro and Gershon were experts in all types of drones! Meanwhile, he asked Eric to use his mountaineering skills to ascend the mountain, bring back some rock samples, and closely survey the mountain's summit. Sam insisted on conducting these preliminary tasks so that we knew precisely where to drill, and to mitigate the risk of landslides. Ariel mentioned that he and Julie would remain here to film the drone's setup and launch, but asked Eric to bring a small portable camera to record anything he deemed significant. He recommended that Eric attach it to his shoulder strap to film while climbing, adding that once set, it would continuously record.

Eric was thrilled with his assignment. He dashed back to our tent to change into long pants, a long-sleeved shirt and a sun cap; then to the supply tent to grab his mountain climbing equipment. He moved too swiftly for me to keep up. He noticed this as he left the supply tent, heading towards our new target mountain. He quickly turned, ran back, planted a kiss on my lips, and said, "See you soon." I understood his meaning perfectly. Not only would I slow him down, but I also suspected that neither he nor Sam would ever let me go mountain climbing again after that fiasco with the cobra! I tracked Eric with my eyes as he jogged across the now bone-dry ancient riverbed towards the site of the homing beacon that Sam had affixed to the rock face, and then when he began circling the mountain to find the ideal starting point for his climb. I watched until he vanished from sight.

Now, the only ones left in camp with nothing to do were Asher and myself. We both made the same decision to walk over and observe Sam and his volunteer helpers set up the drone and the computer equipment needed to control it. Twenty minutes later, we all heard a muted shout. It was Eric, waving from the mountain top! Naturally, we all waved back. I commented on his speed, to which Sam responded, "Not surprising. Eric climbs like a mountain goat."

About an hour later, we all spotted Eric as he jogged back to us. Upon arrival, he announced his mission had been successful. The reason for his quick return, he explained, was that he had discovered an ancient rock trail cut into the backside of the mountain leading to the top. Though parts were unusable, most of it expedited his ascent and descent considerably. That, he continued, was the good news. The not-so-good news was that the side of the mountain facing Mount Karkom, the side where the rainbow had guided us, displayed signs of a major ancient landslide. Moreover, the rock samples he had gathered at the top, which he now showed us, were composed of a type of limestone that crumbled easily. In his estimation, there was a substantial risk of another possible landslide. Sam listened intently and suggested we await the drone's findings. However, Eric had one more matter to discuss.

He slowly took a breath. He began that while finding an ancient rock cut trail to the top was certainly intriguing, there was something even more so. He had found cut marks hammered into the edge of the mountain top above where the landslide had occurred. In other words, this landslide on the side of the mountain appeared to be man-made. Asher interrupted Eric by saying that was very improbable and unprovable. In response, Eric showed us the photos he had taken of a stone hammer and a piece of very sharp, hand-held granite—an ancient Egyptian technique used to carve rock. Both were found near one of the cut scars at the edge of the mountain top. And if that wasn't enough, he then removed and unwrapped the same items from his backpack, matching those in the photos. Eric continued, suggesting that carbon dating of the wood in the handle of the stone hammer would reveal approximately when this man made landslide had occurred. The team took a collective breath during his presentation. This was a puzzling and astounding discovery. Eric returned the camera to Ariel so he could promptly upload the photos and videos of Eric's expedition to the cloud as a permanent record.

Asher thought he was going to have the last word when he reminded Eric that no one was permitted to remove artifacts from their place of discovery by Israeli law. Therefore, he had effectively violated the law. Had he directed this comment towards me, I would have been tempted to slug him, taking the satisfaction of breaking his jaw before landing in jail.

However, Eric responded calmly but firmly that Asher was correct, artifacts are not permitted to be removed unless photographs and videos were extensively taken of the artifacts "in place" including measurements to nearby landmarks before their removal. He added that upon scrutinizing the photographs and videos, you will find all this was done before I carefully removed the items. Mark couldn't resist chiming in, telling Asher that he should get his facts straight before he spoke next time.

CHAPTER 9

IT IS TIME!

After that somewhat tense moment, Sam told the team, "Let's rev up the drone and get it airborne to see what we can find!" Our young helicopter crew members, Jethro and Gershon, were ready to launch the drone. Sam gave them a hand sign, and up and away it went. No matter how many times I had seen a drone fly, it still gave me a thrill. Our small drone was essentially a mini unmanned helicopter. However, I sometimes felt a little fear and anxiety about something that could be potentially uncontrollable and dangerous. But this was certainly not the case with our drone, deftly managed by Sam and his two very knowledgeable volunteer helpers. It ascended rapidly and headed directly for our target mountain. There, it hovered above the mountain for a few minutes, taking ground-penetrating radar images as Sam had outfitted it with a GPR unit. It then began to make small circles in the air that grew larger, photographing more and more area of the mountain. Then, at the largest circle circumference, it backtracked, retracing its route flying smaller and smaller circles. It did this three times. This took about two hours to complete. After completing the mission, it flew back and landed exactly where it was supposed to land—in front of us. I knew I shouldn't have felt this way, but I was relieved when it landed and that slight buzzing noise it made ceased. This new technology can sometimes be unsettling to me. (In the back of my mind I thought it looked and sounded like a big black wasp!) Of course, the team was elated when it landed, and everyone broke into applause for Sam, Jethro, and Gershon for a job well done.

We all followed Sam into the mess tent so, under the shade, we could better see what the radar had revealed. Sam saw it first, and with a big smile, announced there was a hollow space inside the mountain—very possibly a cave or room! We all crowded around his computer as he explained how to interpret the radar images on his screen. Everyone in the tent was ecstatic, everyone except Asher, who turned sullen. I always kept half an eye on him.

Sam called the room to order as he said we needed to figure out our next steps. Eric chimed in that we had to determine how to get in there without the rest of the mountain falling on us! Sam shared that he had something else to add. He reminded us of our first day here when we tried to discover if there was a cave or room inside Mount Karkom based on my suspicion that there was an ancient road leading into the side of Mount Karkom. He then broke the news that the aerial GPR had picked up the same ground indentations as the supposed road but on the opposite side of the river, leading directly into the side of this new mountain we were now exploring. Everyone turned and looked at me. All I did was smile, throw up my hands and say, "Hey, I love it when a plan comes together!"

Sam rapped his knuckles on the table to refocus everyone on our next steps. He continued that according to the GPR images, the thinnest wall inside the mountain cavity was on the side facing the burning bush phenomenon on Mount Karkom. In other words, the ground indentations were probably guiding us to what was the ancient mountain cavity entrance. However, it would take at least a week of careful digging to clear the entrance from the landslide debris. I interjected that if we had a bulldozer and used it carefully, we could cut that time to one day, and it might even come in handy in case of another landslide.

The tent erupted into shouting matches between team members over my bulldozer idea. Sam yelled for everyone to quiet down so we could discuss this sensibly. Asher spoke first, asserting this was a World Heritage classified site and shouldn't be touched, and a bulldozer might cause another landslide. Sam responded that we already had permission to dig here and use any appropriate equipment. Eric added that once we obtained a bulldozer, we could drive it from its delivery site on the nearby military air base using the dry riverbed right up to the cave entrance, minimizing any damage to the terrain. Then Jethro, one of the young helicopter crewmen, raised his hand to speak. He informed us that we would need a mini bulldozer, also called a compact bulldozer, for this job. He had experience driving one many times before and volunteered for the task. He also knew there was a mini bulldozer available at the Hatzor Air Base.

I naively asked how we would transport it here. Jethro explained, in the respectful tone of a teenager explaining to a parent how to use an iPhone for the first time, that the Chinook helicopter could airdrop the bulldozer in front of the cave entrance and retrieve it the same way when ready, causing minimal damage to the terrain. That settled the debate in my mind. All I said was I needed to call Jacob to update him, which I did. After my call with Jacob, I asked Sam to please set the wheels in motion with the military to get the bulldozer here as soon as possible. Sam made a call and afterward told everyone that the bulldozer would arrive within two hours. We ended the meeting when Asher announced that a quick light lunch was ready. I thought to myself that things certainly move fast in Israel when you know the right people!

The mini bulldozer arrived right on time. I was fascinated to watch the logistics of the Chinook helicopter landing it just about fifty feet in front of where we needed to start clearing the landslide debris. It was dropped with almost pinpoint accuracy with the help of Jethro and Gershon, our two helicopter crewmen who directed the pilot from the ground and unwrapped the mini bulldozer as it landed with a thud. Jethro immediately checked it over and yelled to everyone as the copter departed that the bulldozer had a full tank of gas and was ready to go. The copter departed, leaving us all coughing due to the large amount of dust its spinning blades kicked up. As the dust cleared, I could see that Eric was already standing by Jethro, who was seated in the bulldozer, giving him last minute instructions. He reminded Jethro that this was not a construction site but a delicate archeological excavation. Eric wanted him to go extremely slowly so he and Sam could examine what was being removed before Jethro dumped it. They both proceeded to examine every bulldozer shovel full of landslide rock and debris. Then, as Jethro backed up the bulldozer to dump it in our designated dump site, they also turned to examine the gap in the landslide debris that the bulldozer had made. This procedure, of course, slowed us down in getting to the actual side of the mountain. While this was happening, Asher and I stood by the side of the pathway being created, our eyes glued to the action. Ariel and Julie filmed everything. Because of the slow process of removing the landslide rock, we worked until sunset that day and adjourned to the next day to finish this stage.

The next morning, Eric was up and out before I awoke. He met Sam, Jethro, and Gershon by the bulldozer at the crack of dawn. Asher brought coffee and Danish pastries to the site for them. Ariel and Julie were there filming too. However, I heard it loud and clear when they turned on the bulldozer engine again. The sound could wake the dead. I immediately woke up, dressed, and met them all at the site. I saw there were half a dozen brooms, shovels, smaller spades, pointed trowels, buckets, etc., lined up against the side of the pathway we had created. Eric and Sam were watching Jethro and the bulldozer very closely to make sure when the bulldozer work needed to stop due to the proximity of the mountainside. That was when the individual physical excavation work would begin, making sure nothing we did damaged the side of the mountain or even scratched it. The good news was that the bulldozer rock removal was proceeding more quickly than yesterday, and so far, there were no new landslides. The bulldozer continued removing rock until late morning when both Sam and Eric agreed that from then on, we had to do the excavation by hand. The bulldozer was backed up and parked at the edge of the dry riverbed.

We all grabbed our excavation tools including myself and Asher and formed a line. At the beginning of the line, which was nearest to the mountain wall still covered in debris, were Eric, Sam, and Asher. They started using shovels to fill buckets or discard small rocks but soon switched to smaller tools. Then Jethro and Gershon would carry the full buckets to me and empty them into grates. When I shook the grates back and forth, it would filter the debris, allowing much of it to fall into other buckets underneath. Jethro and Gershon would then empty those buckets when they became full. I was tasked to look for anything that might be considered an ancient relic or be useful to our search, and put it aside for the two trained archeologists to further examine what I had found. Unfortunately, I found nothing sifting rock and dirt all day except for one thing, and that turned out to be a stupendous discovery. It was a small piece of gold, the size of a small rock that could be easily held in the palm of one hand. When I gave it to Eric for examination, he immediately recognized the cartouche of Pharaoh Tutankhamun faintly carved on one side of it.

He explained to all of us that in the 17th Dynasty of ancient Egypt, circa 1350 BCE, coins were not used as a medium of exchange. It was primarily a barter system of trade. However, gold, silver, and copper were also used in trade. Therefore, this rock with the cartouche of the king carved on it meant that this was the king's gold. Holding it in the palm of his hand, he estimated that this little rock was priceless and a monumental archeological discovery, begging the question of what it was doing in the middle of the Negev. I asked Ariel to make sure he filmed this small gold rock from several different angles. Eric then put it in a plastic bag and into his buttoned breast pocket for safekeeping.

Less than thirty minutes after the discovery of the small gold Egyptian rock, the team hit a wall made of perfectly cut large limestone blocks. After our discovery of the gold rock, this was the second time that day we were all astounded and excited. We hurriedly used our brooms to brush away the final dust and debris that covered this newly discovered wall. This revealed a wall of cut stone about fifteen feet (4.6m) high and about twenty feet (6.1m) wide. Each stone was perfectly fitted to the others and were about two feet (.6m) wide by four feet (1.2m) long. It looked like it had been built to block the entrance to a natural cave. We went from excitement to complete silence while we studied our discovery, trying to figure out what it was hiding and who built it and why.

I spoke first (of course) when I said it looked to me like whoever built this wall certainly knew what they were doing. In fact, because of the quality of workmanship, it had to have been built by master stonemasons and cutters. Everyone turned to look at me when I added, "It took the kind of expertise that former Hebrew slaves would have acquired constructing monuments in Egypt for the Pharaoh." And before anyone said anything, I added, "I also just came to the conclusion that the reason we did not find anything except a blank wall and a solid mountain across the river during our first exploratory endeavor was that what we were looking at was a quarry for these stones. And the tracks I thought I saw leading into Mount Karkom were actually leading away from it to the other side of the ancient river. They were actually drag marks on the ground made by these heavy stones being placed here." Eric then added that the wall was missing a doorway or entrance. Therefore, in his opinion, this wall was meant to permanently seal what lay inside especially since someone had also taken the trouble of hiding it under a manmade landslide.

Not surprisingly, Asher shook his head in disbelief. Moreover, he said my theory was just a theory that could not be proved. I responded that I knew my hunches were sometimes provocative but I felt they were missing the most important point. It was plain to me that the stone blocks we saw in front of us because their color was saffron and very different then the color of the surrounding limestone came from a quarry cut from Mount Karkom across the dry riverbed. The color of Mount Karkom was also saffron. Indeed, the name in Arabic, Jabal Ideid, for this mountain translates to Mountain of Saffron. And I also believed that Mount Karkom was Mount Sinai, God's sacred mountain. So, if I was correct, then the real question was why bother using stones from that far away when there was perfectly good limestone that could be cut and used much closer to this location? Why was sacred stone used to seal this opening? My hunch was that someone was making a point. Perhaps it was Moses? Although, why, we did not know yet.

Sam interjected that it was getting late and that we should stop for the day. We all agreed that it had been a very exciting day and there was much to think about and discuss. Asher said he needed to hurry back to get dinner ready and that he was going to break out extra wine tonight, adding that we all deserved it.

Eric and I were the stragglers walking back to the tent for dinner. Ever since I sprained my ankle, I was walking a little slower, especially over the uneven river stones. Eric let me set our pace. As we slowly walked back, I turned to him and asked if he thought I was going crazy with my new hunches about what happened here over three thousand years ago. He put his right arm around my shoulders and gave me a slight hug. Then he surprised me by resting his head on my shoulder for a minute. When he did this, I assumed he was being kind because he really believed I was nuts. But I misread him. With his head on my shoulder, he firmly said that the evidence was mounting that I was a hundred percent correct. His confidence in me renewed my faith in myself and our love for each other. I was ready for the next day.

I slept somewhat later the next day. I guess I needed it. When I looked over to the cot beside me where Eric slept, he was gone. I didn't think much of it then because I knew Eric liked to work out early in the morning. However, as I walked over to wash at what passed for our sink and shower area, I noticed Ariel standing with his back to our tents filming something in the distance. As I walked closer to him, he turned and said he had just caught this action. I thought to myself, "What action?" Then I turned to look at what he was filming. It was Eric dangling on a rope halfway down the cliffside of Mount Karkom about where I was the other day. As I focused, I saw Eric begin to rappel down the mountainside the rest of the way to the ground where Sam was waiting for him. He then unhitched his harness and jerked the rope three times. This caused both his mountain climbing rope and pulley to fall down the cliffside, landing about ten feet from them. Next, they folded the rope and picked up the pulley apparatus and came walking quickly back to where I was. Two thoughts raced through my mind. First, "What the heck were they doing and why?" And second, I had not realized how unstable the pulley holding the rope was. So, I decided in that instant to never go rappelling down a mountain again! And it also made me worry about Eric's safety to watch him do this.

By now the rest of the team had become aware of what was happening and had gathered around us waiting for them to return. Eric and Sam both nonchalantly said, "Shalom" when they greeted us. Then Eric added, "What a great way to start the day!" As he greeted us like this, I thought to myself that it was so dangerous what he had just done. But I said nothing. Sam added that Eric had some very interesting news to share. Apparently, Eric explained, the other landslide above the first area we explored was also manmade. He said he had found six slice marks in the limestone that were manmade and could definitely cause a slide. He took photos of them and it was his opinion that they were the same as the marks he found at our other site. Then Eric looked straight at me and said loud and clear that this was another step closer to proving my theories as to what happened here three thousand years ago. Everyone looked at me and clapped. I was elated that my husband was helping me prove my hunches. All I said in response was that it was indeed a great way to start the day and all before breakfast too! Moreover, I added I thought these two deserved as a reward an extra five minutes each to shower this morning! Everyone laughed and applauded and wholeheartedly agreed.

After breakfast was finished, Sam held another strategy meeting for the team. The big question at the meeting was how to proceed to look inside the sealed mountain cavity without damaging anything or causing another landslide. Both Ariel and Sam agreed that we should use the same technique we used previously when we drilled into the buried room that contained King Herod's treasure. This involved Sam drilling a small hole through the stone into the cavity beyond. The hole would be big enough to fit Ariel's endoscopic camera, commonly called a snake cam, which was attached to the front of a long tube snaked through the drilled hole. The head of the snake cam had the ability to light up the space and turn 180 degrees while filming. This would give us a well-lit, sweeping view of what was inside. Sam also said we might have to drill more than one spot to see everything we needed. Additionally, the snake cam would be hooked up to a laptop computer which Ariel could monitor. Sam said that it was safer to do it this way first to avoid any problems. Or in other words, we could see where we needed to go. In anticipation of a need like this, both Sam and Ariel had brought all the necessary equipment with them.

When we arrived at our site in front of the very precisely cut limestone blocks sealing the opening facing Mount Karkom, Sam had to make an important decision: where to drill our first hole? By tapping the stone blocks with the blunt end of his big knife, he tried to determine the most structurally sound spot to drill. He found a spot towards the left side of the sealed opening, close to the natural wall. He chose a spot that was at the corner junction of two stones, at a height of about four feet (1.2m) off the ground (or two stone levels). So, even though the stones were fitted perfectly tightly together, there was already a cut space separating the stones at the point he chose. Sam used a portable motor to power his drill. It took almost an hour to cut through what turned out to be two feet (.6m) of thick stone. He mentioned that usually the drill could cut limestone much faster, but he drilled extremely slowly so the vibrations would not cause another landslide. After he finished drilling into a space that had not been seen for more than three thousand years, a small mound of saffron colored limestone dust lay piled on the floor below the new hole.

Now it was Ariel's and Julie's turn. Ariel pushed the snake cam through the new silver dollar sized hole until it emerged at the other end. Julie was seated on a small wooden stool, looking intently at a computer sitting on an equally small aluminum table. The computer displayed and recorded everything the snake cam was filming. Ariel held the tube attached to the camera to steady it. Everyone crowded around Julie and the computer to catch a glimpse of what the camera was filming. It was startling. The light from the camera as it slowly turned 180 degrees back and forth revealed a very large natural cave with what seemed to be dozens of skeletons lying on the ground. Many of them seemed to be piled in the center of the cave. Everyone had their turn to look at the computer to see what was inside. I noticed the entire team had gone silent. Everyone was trying to figure out what we had just discovered.

Finally, Sam said it was time to drill another hole to confirm everything. This time it was at the corner junction of two stones located in the center of the wall. The same steps performed to drill the first hole were repeated to drill the second hole. Except this time, Julie was the first to notice there were what seemed to be carved or painted inscriptions on the right side wall of the cave. Everyone got a turn to look. And everyone had questions about the inscriptions. However, Ariel emphatically said that his camera was not made to pick up that kind of detail from this distance and if we wanted to read what was written on the wall, we would have to enter the cave to do so. Of course, this added to everyone's excitement and confusion as to what lay inside. However, it was now obvious to the whole team that we were dealing with a natural cave whose entrance had been sealed. It was also obvious that this was some sort of tomb. But everything else about it was still an open question. By this time, it was getting late in the day and Sam called off further exploration until the next day. We all had a great deal to think about, except for me: I had a hunch as to exactly what we discovered. But I was reluctant to say anything since, if I was correct, then Asher would have the expedition shut down. I decided that I would have to manage this discovery extremely carefully going forward to avoid trouble with Asher or the government.

At dinner that night the main topic of conversation was our new discovery. Everyone had their own opinion as to what we were going to find when we opened it. The second topic of discussion was just how we were going to open it. There was much talk and drinking of good Israeli wine. However, I said nothing—just listened. And Asher, too, said nothing—just listened. We both sensed that our main battle over the future of our expedition and any new discoveries would commence soon. I also believed that Sam and Eric were both aware of the possibility of a theological biblical war emanating from our expedition discoveries. New evidence that could prove, change, or refute the Book of Exodus!

However, at our strategy meeting after breakfast the next day, the team's main concern was how to get into the cave-like room without the mountain collapsing on us. After much discussion, Sam offered his solution: We would use one of his stone cutting saws to cut a hole big enough in the limestone for a man to walk through. Almost at the same time that we cut a space open, we would need to replace and brace it with a strong wooden support beam. Because we would cut a little deeper each time as we cut out a section of stone, we would need to use several vertical wooden support beams on each side of the cut. Also, the lintel, which was the top support beam, would be made from several wooden beams laid next to each other as we removed stone sections cut deeper into the blocks. The first cut would be the most difficult to remove. So he recommended we cut it into small pieces, removing the small pieces of the block one at a time making a carved out square area. The rest of the opening was going to be easier to cut but far more dangerous due to the larger and deeper size of the opening leading to a stronger possibility of a landslide or wall collapse. After we got our door cut and braced, we could determine at a later date if it might not be a better idea for safety reasons to take the entire wall down. In anticipation of something like this, he had already brought all the supplies and equipment needed. Sam needed two volunteers to help him with this very dangerous project of simultaneously cutting and building a doorway into this ancient wall.

In fact, it was going to be so dangerous that he wanted everyone working on cutting the door to wear hard hats and a rope around their waists in case they needed to be pulled out from under a landslide. He then asked for volunteers to help him. Eric immediately raised his hand, as did I. Sam immediately accepted Eric but declined my offer. He flat out told me I was too old for this project. Before I could respond, Jethro volunteered and Sam accepted him. I was crushed. To placate me, Eric explained that what Sam meant to say was that I was too valuable to the expedition. They all could tell that I was not happy. But I responded by insisting on being the first person to enter the cave. The entire team went silent, but finally, Sam and the entire team agreed to my request. Then I turned to Ariel and Julie and told them that I thought they should use the type of camera lens that allowed them to stand as far back as possible to keep them out of danger. We ended the strategy meeting when I said I would be the one holding the other end of those ropes tied around everyone's waists. And at the first sign of trouble, I was going to pull so hard they would be yanked back to Tel Aviv. Both Asher and Gershon would also be standing beside me to help pull the ropes or dig free anyone buried as quickly as possible.

It took about two hours for the team to assemble all the equipment needed and carry it close to our newly discovered stone wall. We even had jugs of water to cool down the drill if it got too hot while drilling through the limestone. Sam started drilling around midday. Oddly, I noticed that this time of year the desert heat was quite welcome since it was December and the daytime temperatures were mildly warm. Moreover, Sam, Eric, and Jethro's first project was to erect a small tent over the spot where they would drill. The top of which was made of heavy aluminum, not to protect them from the heat of the sun, but to further protect them from any falling rocks. They then put on their goggles and hard hats and got started. The drill was a six-inch (15.2cm) round saw that spun around like an axel of a car wheel going 200 miles(322km) an hour. When they started to drill, there was flying saffron colored limestone dust everywhere. And the sound and vibrations of the drill were loud and unnerving. Sam and Eric took turns drilling while Jethro made sure the motor for the drill was running while clearing the area of rock chips. He also handed Eric and Sam water jugs to pour on the drill when it overheated.

As Sam predicted, the first section of the wall to be opened was the slowest to cut. It had to be cut out one small piece at a time. To complicate matters, when the hole had finally been opened, Sam motioned for everyone to move back. He could smell that the air escaping from inside was definitely bad, perhaps even poisonous, and it would take at least twelve hours to dissipate.

"No more drilling today," he announced. "We will start again tomorrow after I determine if the air is safe." He told us that he did not think we needed any security near the wall that night because there was no one else within fifty miles, and also, if someone managed to get into the tomb, the air would probably kill them. He further explained that sometimes noxious gases build up in spaces that have not been exposed to oxygen for a long time. So then, the toxic air had to cycle out for the inside air to normalize.

Even though the rest of the team, including myself, were standing more than twenty feet away from the drilling, we were all covered in saffron dust at the end of the day. Ariel said he had to change his camera lenses three times that day and Julie complained that this saffron color clashed with her red hair! As for our three drillers, the only normal-colored skin that could be seen on them was when they removed their hard hats and goggles. All else was the color of saffron.

We decided to leave all the equipment and the tent where they were. I gave Eric a hug and called him my saffron husband, which made him smile. Even though I realized we all needed a break from the desert, I also knew the excitement of being so near to making a major archeological discovery kept everyone on their toes and moving forward.

As we all began to walk back to our campsite, I took Ariel and Eric aside for a short meeting. I told Ariel that I also wanted Eric to hear my concerns. I continued, saying that I wanted Ariel and Julie in the cave as quickly as possible when it was safe to do so. I wanted them recording everything because I believed that what we may discover in there might not support the orthodox view of the story of the Exodus. Therefore, Asher might want to not only shut down our expedition but also have the cave sealed. But before that happened, I wanted a complete photographic and video record of what we found. Eric agreed that Asher, through the Chief Rabbinate's political influence, could do it or at least slow further exploration and study for a decade or more. Ariel agreed that he and Julie would be on top of it. He also reminded us that everything he filmed or photographed went directly to the cloud, where it was beyond censorship. Nevertheless, he would have his staff in his Tel Aviv studio download everything to multiple places for security. Now, as we made our way back to our tents, I also called Jacob to update him and alert him about the possible "Asher" problem. He was delighted with our dig's progress and thanked me for the heads up.

The next morning the entire team rose early, ate early, and was assembled and ready to start at our site outside the ancient wall. Sam said he had to test the air coming from the newly opened hole in the wall. He would use a military grade handheld air quality monitor that would test the air for impurities, or with a smile on his face, we could do it the old-fashioned way. By that he meant one of the team members could walk over, stick his head in the hole and take a deep breath. If he died, we would know we needed to wait a little longer for the tomb's toxic air to normalize. If he didn't die, then we could proceed. No one laughed at this except Sam. I thought to myself, he had such a dark sense of humor.

Sam then proceeded to check the air quality three times. First, he put his handheld monitor just outside the hole in the wall, then halfway inside the hole, and finally, he stretched his arm holding the device as far as it would go through the hole inside the tomb. Each time the air quality monitor registered clean. He then turned to us and said, "It's safe. Let's cut this baby open!".

The team reassembled itself as they had on the previous day, with one difference. Today, Sam used a much larger round drill saw. The larger saw cut through the limestone wall like it was butter. Jethro spent most of his time pouring water over the drill to keep it from overheating and also trying to wet the dust so it would not fly all over the place. Eric was very busy trying to slip pre-cut pieces of wood into the opening to brace it. They only stopped to custom cut the wooden braces when they didn't exactly fit. It took them almost four hours, but when they were done, we had a doorway that a full grown man could walk through! And with no landslides—so far! We all helped remove the heavy stone debris created from this new opening by pushing the stones far enough away so our bulldozer could pick it up and dump it.

It was just past lunchtime when the doorway was finished, but everyone was so excited that no one was hungry. We did, however, have a good supply of bottled water with us, so we were all sufficiently hydrated. I even carried my canteen full of water on my utility belt, which I had filled from the river the other day.

The drillers took off their hats and goggles. We all got our flashlights ready. Then, I walked up to the doorway entrance, took Eric by the hand and we entered the tomb together with our flashlights on high. I had a hunch that both Eric and myself had to be the first ones to enter this tomb. I felt deeply that this was both a sacred and profane place at the same time and that we both were somehow chosen to be the ones to enter first. Asher insisted on being next to enter, reminding everyone that he was supposed to ensure that there would be no desecration of any sacred Jewish objects and that we all observed all Israeli archeological laws. Sam also reminded everyone not to touch anything. After Asher had entered, Ariel, Julie, and Sam followed. Sam asked Jethro and Gershon to remain outside for now for two reasons: First, there were already too many people in the cave to control and ensure there were no accidents, and second, for safety reasons, he wanted someone outside the cave just in case there was a landslide, so there would be someone there to get help. When Sam entered, he set up a six foot(1.8m) tripod lamp with a self-contained light on the top which helped illuminate the cave. My first comment inside the cave was that this place was huge—much bigger than it seemed on our video camera and it gave me an eerie foreboding feeling. Everyone agreed that they also felt the same sinister aura of the place. Next, Sam firmly told us that we all had to be very careful where we walked. Asher added, "Touch nothing!" Very soon after we entered, all our attention was drawn to the center pile of skeletons which was about five or six feet(1.8m) high.

The main pile was surrounded by more skeletons spreading out about twenty feet(6.1m) in a circular fashion. Some of the skeletons had a big hole in their heads while others were missing their heads completely. Eric said it looked like all these people had been executed. But the strangest thing we noticed was that our flashlights reflected what seemed like gold dust covering the center pile of skeletons. Next, the most fascinating discovery of all was the inscription carved on the right wall of the cave-like tomb. Eric, our linguist, was especially interested in these. According to him, it looked like there were three different languages all written next to each other and possibly all saying the same thing. Each inscription measured approximately the same width and length—about one foot(.31m) wide by three feet(.9m) long—each separated on the wall by about three inches(7.6cm). The language in column on the right side was definitely written in Egyptian hieroglyphics. Moreover, Eric recognized the other languages which he thought were Proto-Canaanite script in the middle column and ancient Akkadian written in cuneiform on the left side column.

According to Eric, based on modern research of Bronze Age languages, Proto-Canaanite was the mother or root language of other languages in later centuries such as Hebrew, Canaanite, and Phoenician. Thus, we were very probably looking at the language in which the Ten Commandments were first written and would have been understood by all the Semitic tribes of the time. Lastly, Akkadian, written in cuneiform, was the most common language in Mesopotamia during the Bronze Age. So the inscriptions on the wall would have been understood in one form or another by the entire Middle East during the Bronze Age. We were all stunned by Eric's explanation of these inscriptions. I had never seen Eric more focused as he studied our new discovery. With all our flashlights focused on these writings, Eric finally turned to us and said he could translate the hieroglyphic inscription.

I could hear Asher gasp when Eric said this. And of course, Ariel and Julie were filming every detail.

Eric started by pointing out the royal cartouche of the Pharaoh Tutankhamun, then pointed to another cartouche which he said no one had ever seen before, but he was almost sure it represented the name of Moses. He pointed to the sign of the Nile River, a basket made of reeds, and a tall staff carved on the cartouche. No one uttered a word or seemed to breathe as Eric continued. He said that this inscription cursed King Tut, the priests of Amun, and the people slain before us in this room. Moses called them followers of Amun and nonbelievers, and the Lord God cursed them for all time. Most astounding was the cartouche that represented the Hebrew God. He was represented as a single burning bush in the center of the cartouche. The whole team took a breath when he showed us this. As he further translated the inscription, I noticed something else. It was the royal cartouche of the Pharaoh Horemheb with which I had become familiar on our trip to Egypt. I specifically noticed it because this cartouche also had the serpent carved into it. In my opinion, this was the real cartouche, like the one I had discovered in Horemheb's tomb. However, I said nothing but wondered why Eric had not mentioned it.

Lastly, Eric concluded that we now have a non-biblical reference to Moses and the Exodus that concurred with the Bible story and gave us an exact timeline of when the Exodus occurred. We knew that King Tut reigned from 1333 BCE to 1323 BCE. So we could now date the Exodus to that timeline. He also added that what lay before us would likely prove to be the Rosetta Stone of the Bronze Age, even if it takes years to fully translate these inscriptions.

Asher then posited that these skeletons must be the remains of the Hebrews who reverted to paganism, whom Moses slaughtered for rejecting the Lord God upon Moses' descent from the mountain. He stated that since they were pagan at the time of their deaths, their bones would not have to be reburied in an Orthodox Jewish cemetery as required by rabbinical law for ancient bones of Jews. Furthermore, he asserted that they were cursed by God. Moreover, he was confident that carbon dating of the bones would indicate their age to be from around 1350 BCE. I suggested that, very probably, the gold dust on the skeletons might be from the golden calf statue that the Bible said Moses ground into dust. With a smile on his face, Asher commended my knowledge of the Bible and opined that our findings here confirmed beyond a shadow of a doubt that Mount Karkom was the Mount Sinai of the Bible. He gave me a big bear hug, exclaiming, "God works in strange ways." He then announced he would begin preparing dinner and intended to leave the following day after breakfast, believing the archeological dig no longer required a rabbi and could proceed without him. He was very pleased that everything here corroborated the Bible story and declared this a discovery of world importance.

When Asher departed the cave, Jethro and Gershon entered with their flashlights to explore and receive updates from us. Eventually, everyone left to freshen up and prepare for dinner, leaving Eric and me alone in this biblical cave-like tomb, which was cursed by Moses himself. Light still shone through our newly created doorway. Tired and thirsty, we sat cross-legged on the floor, leaning against the rear wall of the cave to rest. As we leaned back, I took a sip of the supposed holy water from my canteen and offered some to Eric before setting it between us. As we rested, we could not help but focus on the macabre dance of the piled and twisted skeletons now bathed in the eeriness of the tripod light and our flash lights bouncing through them. However, I could also feel our very real love for each other eclipsing the sinister atmosphere. Ignoring our surroundings, I casually mentioned to Eric that the discovery of this new Rosetta Stone of the Bronze Age would make him a world famous archeologist. Eric remained silent, so I inquired how an archeologist and linguist of his caliber could overlook such an extremely important cartouche as the one for the Pharaoh Horemheb? He smiled and said, "You noticed that. Did you? My partner is so clever." Unsatisfied, I pressed, "That doesn't really answer my question." He then explained that the inscription, in addition to cursing the skeletal remains of the pagans before us, actually praised King Tut as a friend and vilified Horemheb as the true culprit. He continued that if he had translated it that way it would have caused a conflict with the Biblical account of the Exodus, which would have roused the ire of religious authorities and potentially led to the shutdown of the dig. Eric flat out told me that my hunch regarding "the players" in the Egyptian palace during the Exodus three thousand years ago was spot on. He knew I would like to hear this and I did. I realized that Eric had managed to avoid not only a major battle with the Chief Rabbinate by his selective translation but major problems with the organized Christian churches and Islamic mosques. He was truly impressive sometimes and I told him so. We also both realized it would take years if not decades to fully and accurately translate all three inscriptions.

I then thought it was a good time to cautiously approach a sensitive subject between us. Using my most persuasive tone, I pointed out that the discoveries here would make him so famous and recognizable that he would be far less valuable to the Mossad. Moreover, we were both financially secure. So maybe it was time for him to retire from the Mossad? There was a pregnant pause. He then turned to me and agreed. With that response we both bent towards each other to embrace and instead spilled my canteen which was still almost full of water over our clothes and the floor. We both stood up quickly shaking off the water. However, I noticed the water on the floor was seeping under the rear cave wall where we had just been leaning. A moment later Eric noticed this too.

We both dropped to our knees and began clearing the dirt from centuries past to reveal a rock floor with grooves in it. The water was disappearing following these grooves along the rock floor, leading to somewhere under the wall. We ran our fingers along the edge of the floor where the stone wall met the stone floor. We then both looked at each other and said in unison, "It's a false wall!" We both started to laugh. Our laughter echoed through the cave-like tomb, filling every crevice, completely dispelling the mystique of the space and making it ours. We had discovered its most coveted secret. I also felt deeply that the laughter born of our pure love banished the curse from this place. And just like that God's curse was lifted. Or, as is said in Africa and the

Caribbean, there was no more bad juju here. We both felt the eerie profanity of this cursed place vanish. I understood now what the Kabbalists meant when they told me, "It is time." I was also deeply aware that the Lord God guided us here to rediscover this place. Spontaneously, I said out loud, "Thank you, God, for sending us this holy water, so we could find this." To which Eric added, "Amen." The very next action Eric took was to unsnap his knife from his belt and tap the wall with the end of its handle. He determined that the bottom of the wall was stone, which produced a hollow sound when tapped, indicating a space behind it. The rest of the upper wall was made from something else that did not produce a hollow sound. It was getting too late for further investigation. So, I said to Eric, "Let's cover up the dirt we just cleared away, turn off the light on the tripod, and get out of the tomb. I need to call Jacob."

Standing outside the doorway of the tomb, I called Jacob and put it on speakerphone so Eric could listen. Before we said anything more than hello, Jacob couldn't stop congratulating us on our discovery that proved Mount Karkom was the real Mount Sinai. He had already seen the film footage that Ariel had taken. He continued to praise us about the skeletons and the Rosetta Stone of the Bronze Age that theologians and archeologists would be studying for years. He expressed his desire to visit the site soon, along with the Director of the Israel Museum, the Director of Israel's Antiquity Authority, and possibly the Prime Minister. Noticing that Eric and I were silent, Jacob's tone changed and became more serious as he asked, "Bring me up to date." I responded by confirming what he said about our discovery but added that Eric and I had just discovered something else, and we needed more time at the site. Jacob took a breath at the other end of the phone. So I continued, revealing that other than myself and Eric, he was the only other person at the moment who knew this. But a few minutes ago, we had discovered the back wall of the cave was a false wall with a hollow space behind it. Furthermore, I informed him that Rabbi Asher Ben-Levy had decided to leave the next day, and we didn't want him to know about this discovery at this point. Let him leave happy. I asked if Jacob could send a helicopter for Asher early the next day, as well as a new cook, preferably one who wasn't kosher. Additionally, I emphasized the importance of delaying any press or high-level visitors until we discovered what lay behind the false wall. Eric suggested that as an excuse for needing more time, Jacob should tell everyone that we needed a little more time to catalog our findings.

I ended with a question, "Is all that possible?"

It took Jacob a minute to process what I had just said, and then he responded affirmatively. He added that everything would be on an early helicopter flight the next day, including his personal chef, whose name was Noah. With that, Jacob ended the call. As we exited the tomb, Eric proceeded to hang a tarp made of plastic in front of the tomb's entrance to prevent bats and the like from entering. Both Eric and I were elated as we walked back to our campsite. However, Eric cautioned me to let him do the talking at dinner that night to avoid raising Asher's suspicions.

We spent some time washing off the telltale dirt from the tomb on our hands and faces before entering the mess tent. We were the last to arrive. As soon as Eric looked at Sam, Sam sensed something had changed. This was reinforced when Eric did all the talking, and I remained silent (unusual for me). The entire team was in high spirits, basking in the glow of our recent discovery. Towards the end of the meal, Eric raised his wine glass and made a toast to our team and especially to Asher, wishing him a safe trip home. Eric informed him that a helicopter had been arranged to pick him up early the next day. During dinner, Sam asked me if I was okay since I seemed less talkative than usual. When I looked him straight in the eye and firmly answered, "Everything was more than fine," he instantly understood my message and knew something was afoot. Shortly afterward, Eric announced that he wanted to stay a bit longer at the dig site to begin cataloging the skeletons and to further study the inscriptions. I said I would stay on as well to help him, and that anyone else who wanted to stay was invited to do so. Everyone raised their hand to stay, except Asher, of course.

The next morning, Asher left on schedule, very early in the morning. As Asher climbed onto the helicopter, Noah, our new cook, jumped off. Asher had been driven to the helicopter landing site on the nearby military training base by both Jethro and Gershon in one jeep. On the return trip, Jethro drove Noah and Gershon drove a second jeep, which he had acquired from the base, loaded with new food supplies. Ariel, of course, filmed Asher's departure and Noah's arrival. When they arrived back at camp, the first thing I noticed about Noah was that he seemed so clean and closely shaved compared to us desert rats. In the mess tent, he told us that before his work as a private chef, he had owned a restaurant and before that cooked for the IDF in the field. He mentioned that the soldiers always told him his food was the best they had ever eaten. Everyone applauded when they heard this. I then welcomed him and mentioned that if he was interested and had the time, he could join us today at our excavation site across the old dry riverbed.

We could always use an extra pair of hands. He responded that he was certainly interested since he was also an amateur archeologist. He also requested an hour to prepare a light breakfast this time since he was unfamiliar with the kitchen. I thought to myself, why am I not surprised that he was interested in helping us? It seems everyone in Israel is an amateur archeologist.

Sam now called a strategy meeting to order while Noah prepared breakfast. Ariel turned his camera on Sam and the meeting. Sam started the meeting by directly asking both Eric and me, "What's going on?" Eric answered that last night before we left the tomb, we had knocked over my canteen filled with river water and it had spilled on the stone floor, which led us to discover that the rear wall of the tomb was a false wall and there was a hollow sounding space behind it. He added that we needed to research this further as soon as possible. When he said this, the team exploded with questions and the energy level in the room noticeably rose.

Sam's first comment was that we would probably have another rabbi down here sooner rather than later because our discovery seriously affected the Exodus story in the Bible. He also mentioned that various Israeli ministries would want to get involved. He recommended we move fast but thoroughly and safely before we lost control over the site.

Eric then asked me if I had a hunch about what was behind the false rear wall. The whole team turned and focused on me. I simply said that I had a very strong hunch about what we were going to discover. Sam pressed me by asking, "Well then, don't keep us in suspense. Please tell us." I thoughtfully responded in the most low key manner that I could muster, that the word "plunder" was mentioned in the Exodus story three times in relation to the gold and silver that the Hebrews took from Egypt. "My question to myself for some time now was: what happened to it?" The whole team fell silent, processing what I had just said.

Noah then suddenly announced that he was ready with biscuits, jams, coffee, and orange juice for breakfast. He said that due to the circumstances, he thought a light, quick breakfast was best for everyone. He was correct. We devoured it and then almost ran to the dig site, including Noah, our newest team member.

When we arrived at the tomb entrance, Sam immediately organized us. He stressed that he did not want everyone in the tomb all at once; first, because too many people might accidentally damage an artifact, and second, there was still a possibility of a landslide and if that happened, he wanted people on the outside to help dig the others out. Eric then proceeded to remove the plastic tarp he had hung the previous night from the entrance to the tomb.

Sam said the first group to enter would consist of himself, Eric, me, Ariel and Julie. Jethro, Gershon, and Noah should wait to enter later.

As we entered the cave, Ariel turned on the tripod light and continued to film everything. We all quickly walked to the rear wall of the cave-like tomb. As we stood in front of the rear wall, Sam mentioned something that I found intriguing. He said that today the tomb felt different, much less ominous than yesterday. Eric and I exchanged glances. How could we tell Sam and the others that with God's help, our love had lifted His curse last night? In response, all I said to Sam was that it must be the morning light that made the place feel different.

Anyway, we were all focused on the rear wall. Eric was the first to realize exactly what we were looking at. He exclaimed that the bottom three feet(.9m) was limestone block, but the rest of the wall to the ceiling was made of mud brick patties. Sam quickly added that this type of construction gave the upper part of the wall a solid, straight base upon which to rest. Eric also added that it was much quicker to construct a wall like this as well. Therefore, Eric continued that, what we were looking at here were genuine mud bricks made by the ancient Hebrews, the same type of mud bricks mentioned in the Bible. Sam then said that this keeps getting better and better. To which I replied, "You haven't seen anything yet. The big enchilada is behind this wall!"

Sam continued that our main problem was twofold: first, how to cut through these bricks without the rest of them collapsing on us, and second, how to do it quickly. He mentioned that we needed to do it fast because if these mud bricks were indeed made under the direction of either Moses himself or Joshua, then this site could become a sacred pilgrimage site for all three monotheistic religions, and we would never be allowed to see what was on the other side. I immediately countered Sam's point when I said that I deeply believed that God led us to this point and He outranks both Joshua and Moses. Eric immediately stepped into our conversation to end it when he said this was not the time or the place for theological arguments. Let's just agree on how we can quickly and successfully penetrate this wall. Julie then spoke and suggested that we put plastic tarps to cover the skeletons and inscription on the wall, and then try to cut into the brick like we did the doorway, bracing it with wood as we go. Sam said that since the mud bricks were not very thick—maybe six to eight inches(20.3cm) deep, he could use his smallest drill to minimize the vibrations and help avoid a collapse. The hole would be drilled into the lowest level of mud brick resting on the limestone rock base. Sam said it would only be a test hole to determine the strength of the mud brick wall and assess the air quality of the space behind the wall. Once we had our plan, the next two hours were spent getting all the equipment together and setting it up in the tomb. In the meantime, the rest of the team got a chance to look around the cave-like tomb and also helped us prepare. Again, when we were ready to drill, Sam and Eric both had ropes tied around them while Gershon, Noah, and myself held the other ends just outside the entrance to the tomb. Ariel stood inside the doorway, filming them—close enough for a good camera shot but also close enough to the doorway to get out quickly in case of trouble. It took us about two hours to properly cover the skeletons with plastic to protect them. Sam had spent most of the two hour prep time studying the wall. Interestingly, this time, Sam also asked Gershon to bring a ladder from our equipment tent. I could tell he had a plan but did not yet know what it was. The tomb's ceiling height in this rear area was about nine feet(2.7m) high while the bottom three feet(.9m) was stone block. The entire length of the mud brick wall was just about twenty feet(6.1m). So, Sam and Eric were dealing with about six feet(1.8m) of piled mud bricks between the ceiling of the tomb and the lower limestone rock wall base. Since the drill was much smaller this time Sam said he did not need someone to pour water on it to cool it when drilling. Also, so much water in the cave could damage other artifacts.

Just before Sam started to drill, I received a call on my cell from Jacob. He said that Asher had held a press conference upon his arrival and had announced that we had discovered a tomb in front of Mount Karkom that proved unequivocally that it was the real Mount Sinai. He also announced that in the tomb there were three Rosetta Stone-like inscriptions, with one of them being the language in which the Ten Commandments were written, and the tomb also contained human skeletons dating back to the Exodus. His press conference had hit Israel and the world like a lightning strike. Jacob continued that first thing tomorrow morning there would be a helicopter arriving with the Prime Minister, the Directors of the Antiquity Authority, Civil Authority (National Parks), Israel Museum, an IDF General, and himself on it. This was our heads-up about tomorrow. All I said before we ended the call was to thank him for the warning and be sure to keep Ariel's film from today in a safe place.

I stopped Sam just before he started to drill and told the whole team what Jacob had just told me. We all agreed that there was a very strong possibility that we would lose control of the site tomorrow if not be escorted off the site completely! So I turned to Sam and said there was no need for test holes. We needed access to the space behind the wall today. He agreed and said he would handle it and asked everyone to return to their respective drilling positions. It was late afternoon when Sam started drilling. After five minutes of drilling a vertical straight line from the middle of the wall down, he then started to climb up the steps on his ladder, extending a straight cutting line up through the mud bricks to the ceiling of the tomb. He yelled to Eric, standing at the foot of the ladder, that his drill was cutting through these mud bricks like a hot knife through butter. Sam then climbed down and moved the ladder a full eight feet(2.4m) along the wall and began the process again. The second straight line of cutting again took almost no time, from the limestone rock base to the ceiling. So now Sam and Eric had two straight cuts going up to the ceiling, about eight feet(2.4m) apart. After this, Sam made two horizontal cuts at the top of the wall closest to the ceiling. His cuts followed the connecting horizontal layers of bricks with a vertical cut between two bricks. He then plucked the cut brick from the wall with his strong fingers and threw it down to Eric who caught it. Each brick weighed about two pounds(.9kg). Eric then laid the brick along the other wall of the tomb opposite the wall with the inscriptions on it. Sam repeated this step several times, creating a square hole about four feet by four feet(1.2m). He then stopped to make sure the air coming out of the hole was good to breathe. He pulled out an air quality testing monitor from his pocket and held it at arm's length inside the hole he had just cut. He waited a couple of minutes for a reading, then yelled to everyone that the air was stale and somewhat foul smelling but safe to breathe. No need to evacuate until tomorrow. Eric yelled up at Sam that he could handle much heavier sections than one brick at a time, so Sam increased the size of the sections he cut and threw to Eric to catch. Very quickly, they finished with the opening in the rear cave wall and called for me to enter it with them. Since it was an eight foot(2.4m) wide cut in the wall, the three of us with our flashlights in hand, and Ariel and Julie filming everything, easily slid over the still existing three foot(.9m) limestone wall. Our flashlights and Ariel's camera light lit up this section of the ancient cave which revealed a dozen large wooden carts set in four rows with three carts in each row with about two feet(.61m) of aisle space between each row. Each cart was loaded with something we could not clearly see at first. This was due to a black coating of dust that covered the top. I simply told Eric and Sam that this was ancient residue from animal skins. As soon as I said this, Eric quickly jerked his head towards me with a quizzical look, as if to ask how and why would I know this? I just responded to his unasked question that DNA testing would confirm what I had just said. Then, to lighten my response a bit, I added that here were also carts made of ancient wood, something archeologists love to find because it's so rare. We all continued to walk down our separate aisles with the ancient wooden carts on either side of us. I was the first to stop and pull out my handkerchief to wipe off the top black layer of residue with several broad swipes, revealing what I already knew. Coincidentally, the very first object I picked up was the golden scepter of King Tut. I immediately noticed the dent in the handle that King Tut had made when he threw it at me in my dream and it had landed on the granite steps leading up to his throne in front of me.

I turned to face Ariel's film camera and announced, "And God said to Moses, 'Plunder the Egyptians of their gold and silver.'" I continued that what we just discovered was "the wealth that was Egypt." And now, I hold in my hand the solid gold scepter of the Pharaoh Tutankhamun, studded with jewels and shaped like a question mark. Further, I added that I have a theory that these wagons, loaded with gold and treasure, moved too slowly when the Hebrews fled Egypt, especially when Moses led the Hebrews from here into the wilderness to avoid pursuit. Wagons pulled by oxen, loaded with gold, could not travel in the rugged wilderness, but neither could chariots in pursuit. So Moses hid the wagons here. Moreover, it was very possible that Moses partially blamed the allure of this treasure for causing the rebellion in the Hebrew camp when the Ten Commandments were being written across the way on Mount Sinai, recently called Mount Karkom. Also, just behind the camera, there were many headless skeletons in the outer room of the tomb that seemed to be covered in gold dust. This was no accident. Lastly, I added that I believe that it was the gold from the golden calf which the Bible said Moses pounded into dust that covered them. And I continued that my guess was that there was so much gold in this place that if it was ever sold, it could balance the budget of the State of Israel.

As I said these things, standing in front of the camera, I felt the penetrating eyes of both Eric and Sam staring at me. I thought to myself that I was glad a wagon load of gold treasure separated them from my show. However, due to their serious stares, I said, as I looked directly at the camera, that I must now put this scepter back exactly where I found it to comply with Israeli law governing archeological sites. After this, Ariel continued to film throughout the new cave room we had just discovered, but I thought I had said enough and it was time to leave.

I met Eric and Sam at the doorway of the tomb entrance. Before they could speak, I said that it was always good to give the audience a little show. But I did not think I had violated any laws? All Sam said in response was, "What part of 'don't touch anything because you're not qualified to do so' didn't you understand?" The next second my cell phone rang. It was Jacob, telling me and the team not to get nervous, but there would be two helicopters arriving very early tomorrow. In addition to the helicopter that carried him and his VIPs, there would be a second one full of IDF soldiers to take control of the site. He then abruptly ended the call.

CHAPTER 10

POSTSCRIPT

It's been nearly a year since our final day in the Negev. Tonight, Eric and I are hosting a dinner party at our place, one of many we've organized since returning. Currently, Eric spends his time writing archeological treatises, delivering lectures to archeologists and theologians, and attending his regular CrossFit gym sessions. Occasionally, he invites me to speak but he complains that I tell too many jokes at the podium and don't take my speaking engagements with these "eggheads" — my term, not his — seriously enough. Interestingly, I always receive a louder applause than him! Moreover, I maintain my belief in the importance of giving the audience a show.

Our buffet dinner party tonight is catered by Noah, who now works for us part-time as a chef, in addition to working for Jacob. Our entire old team, plus Jethro, an invaluable assistant from our last dig who remains a valued member of our team, is here tonight.

During the meal, while we were all discussing current events, I noticed Jacob chuckling to himself after glancing at a piece of art on the wall. So I asked Jacob what he found so amusing. His response was, "Every time I see King Tut's scepter hanging on the wall inside an air tight, bullet proof glass case it makes me chuckle at your audacity and luck. That morning at the Negev dig site, when the Prime Minister thanked you and the team while standing in front of me and all the Directors for a second major Israeli archeological discovery and asked if there was anything he could do for you; you took him up on it. You asked the government to cover all the costs of the expedition, and requested to keep King Tut's scepter which you'd just discovered, on loan from the State of Israel until your death while also promising it would never leave the country. Your request caught me off guard, and his agreement to it stunned me even more. Of course, it helps that the current value of the gold discovered exceeds a billion dollars!"

I replied, "To be honest, I thought there was an equal chance that the Prime Minister would have me arrested for violating Israeli archeological laws." It then struck me to ask Ariel his thoughts on the royal scepter. Ariel immediately mentioned his relief at having filmed the meeting with the team and the Prime Minister, ensuring that the Prime Minister couldn't backtrack on the agreement regarding the scepter. However, he also shared that the most memorable moment he filmed during our expedition was when he interviewed all the team members post-expedition sitting together in a group. The candid conversation, where everyone spoke about their unique experiences at the dig site, stunned the world when I so truthfully answered his question about how I knew where to dig by explaining my dreams and metaphysical relationship to connections with Moses and King Tut and, of course, my unwavering belief that God guided me through signs from the start, especially intrigued audiences. Ariel believed that my account significantly contributed to the success of his film. So much so, he announced, that his documentary about our expedition had gained immense popularity on streaming channels and had just been nominated in the Oscar category for Best Documentary Film of the Year! The entire table erupted in applause.

Next, not to be outdone by Ariel's announcement, Julie stood up at the table and shared that she had just found out a couple of days ago that she was pregnant! The team went wild, standing to hug her and wish her good luck and Mazel Tov!

Once everyone had calmed down and retaken their seats, I turned to Sam to ask for his thoughts when he looked at the scepter. He merely said that after he'd cut open the mud brick wall and seen my performance handling the scepter in front of the camera he thought that there was a strong possibility of some sort of legal punishment. But he is very, very happy it hadn't ended that way!

Finally, I asked Eric, who was seated next to me, what he thought when he looked at the scepter. Eric just looked straight into my eyes and said when he looks at it he is just glad that our honeymoon is not over. With that he reached out to hold my hand. Indeed, I understood what he meant. There isn't a corner of this house in which we haven't made love since we returned. The celibacy that had enveloped us at the sacred mountain had vanished. Moreover, I also had a vague suspicion that our lack of intimacy was one of the reasons that God allowed us to be the first to enter his cursed tomb. But, I could not prove it and therefore will never mention it.

Lastly, the entire table wanted to know what went through my mind when I looked at the scepter. I paused for a long moment. I couldn't reveal that my dream at King Tut's court felt so intensely real to me that I could still picture the King's face as he hurled the scepter at me, or hear the sound it made when it struck the granite steps before me. I couldn't repeat that in my dream, I was there when the dent in the handle was made, and that King Tut intended to give it to me 3500 years ago. So in effect, I was taking back that which was already mine! I didn't want to broach this topic again, as I had done in Ariel's interview, and because I was still uncertain if they all didn't secretly think I am crazy. Therefore, all I said was that Asher was correct when he hugged me and said, "God works in mysterious ways."

With a half smile, Jacob asked, "So, have you had any more metaphysical dreams since returning from Mount Karkom, now called Mount Sinai?" I replied that I hadn't had any such dreams, but I did have a new hunch.

Everyone paused and listened intently to my next words. They all knew what my hunches meant! So I continued that I had recently been studying the Copper Scroll. At the mention of the Copper Scroll, I could sense a collective intake of breath around the table.

I proceeded to explain that, as they all knew, a scroll inscribed on copper was found among the famous Dead Sea Scrolls, hidden in a cave at Qumran. It was unlike the others which were penned on parchment. This scroll allegedly mapped the hiding place of the Temple treasure, stashed away by the Temple Priests before the Romans sacked and destroyed the Temple in 70 CE. To read it, it was unrolled by cutting it into twenty-three strips which laid side by side created a Temple list or accounting of 63 very specific locations and the amount of gold and silver found at each spot. I also studied the unsuccessful expeditions that attempted but failed to locate the treasure. This coupled with the fact that Rome found enormous amounts of gold and silver still in the Temple when they looted it, led many people to believe it was a fake—a decoy to mislead the Romans. My hunch, however, is that they hadn't deciphered the scroll correctly.

A few days ago, while shaving and looking in the mirror, I saw my large photograph of the Copper Scroll's 23 strips lying on my bed. I also noticed that the mirror had reversed the engraved Hebrew letters. So just for fun, I walked over to the photograph and started to play with its position looking at it from different angles. Then on a hunch, I looked at another photograph which showed the back of the scroll. We have to remember that writing on copper creates engraved indentations in reverse on the back side. This is when I noticed that certain engraved letters were so deep into the copper that they pierced the copper forming a very small hole at the bottom of the Hebrew letter. Looking at the back of the scroll I then observed that these small holes no bigger than a pin prick formed straight lines when connected. But my biggest surprise came when I noticed that the three lines converged on very specific Hebrew words that were on the front side of the scroll. I believed these words describe a landmark inside a town. The other end of the lines had names of three towns with Jerusalem being the town at the end of the line in the middle. I then took a map of Judea and Samaria circa 70 CE and overlaid these lines onto the map using Jerusalem as the start point from the middle line. Bingo! All three pointed to a town that still exists today, a place none of the previous expeditions had examined. In other words, in the past everyone has been searching in the wrong places! So, I think we should go look for this Temple treasure.

Jacob and the entire team immediately shouted, "We're in!"

ABOUT THE AUTHOR

Mark Akst is retired and lives in Fort Lauderdale, Florida. *The Secrets of the Saffron Mountain* is his second novel in a series. His professional career included managing hotels in several US cities. He has travelled extensively in North America, Europe and the Middle East. His passionate hobbies are archeology and history. He has a Bachelor of Arts degree from the University of Pennsylvania and an MBA from New York University. All his novels were written for his readers as a fun escape in a stressful world. Visit him at markakst.com